CLOWN WILLIAM

And the Wind of Vengeance

Robin Elno

IE Snaps
by
IngramElliott

Dedication

*For my family, the San Antonio Writers' Guild,
and the wonderful folks at IngramElliott Publishing.*

Wind of Vengeance

An isolated cabin in the New Mexico wilderness, February 1878

A bullet splintered the wood window casing of the cabin where William waited to kill Jesse Evans. William ducked lower. Things had not gone as planned, though one of Jesse's men lay dead on the snow-covered ground a few yards in front of the cabin. Jesse hid in the tree line fifty yards away, cracking away with his rifle at William.

"You're a damn fool, William," Jesse shouted and fired again. "I know you're fast, but a six-gun against a rifle?"

"This d-d-day has been coming for three years." William watched the trees, trying to spot Jesse's position. "Hoot. Ever since you first put a gun in my hand."

"Seems more like God's act than mine," Jesse bellowed. "He's the one made you defective with your jerks and mumbles. It was me helped you discover the gift that came with that curse."

"It is no gift." William fired at the trees. "I hate being a gunfighter. But you and God made it so I have no other choice. I despise you both for it."

"Your hatred addled your brain. You let yourself be caught under my gun like this." A shot, the bullet digging another splinter from the cabin wall, punctuated the statement.

The muzzle flash marked a spot in the trees, creating a perfect target for the next time Jesse fired—provided the outlaw didn't shift to a new spot. William goaded him into another shot. "Your men killed my friend. You drove away my girl, Emily. Sheek, poot. You ruined my chances for a real home in Lincoln."

"Well, when it comes to killin', your Regulator pals ain't any better. How many of Brady's men have they killed? And locked Sheriff Brady up in his own jail. This war ain't personal. Hell, I offered you a job on my side."

"This is personal. I am not riding with those murdering Regulators now. This is about me f-f-finding a place to settle down, in peace."

"Why're you gunnin' for me?"

"Because God is out of my reach."

"And so am I." A muzzle flash just where it had been before.

William snap fired.

And waited.

The sun climbed the sky, and the branches of the trees shed their white sleeves. Ice crystals glistened in the receding snow banks. The air lay still and cold as the top of a frozen stream. The dead man he'd shot that morning sprawled in front of the cabin. The man's horse stood in the open, its head down, nuzzling snow aside as it pulled at tufts of dry grass.

The waiting dragged on. Was there some way to draw Jesse out? With one eye on the tree line, William threw a side of bacon onto the griddle of the potbelly stove heating the rough-hewn cabin. A pot of coffee simmered beside it—a nice welcoming scent to torment a cold and hungry man. He hoped it would make Jesse act rashly. Come and get it, William thought, revolver ready in his hand.

The bacon crisped and the coffee boiled. Jesse did not take the bait.

William ate the bacon and drank the coffee.

There had been no more shots. All was quiet. Too quiet.

Playing the Odds

William peered out the window. No movement in the trees. He slipped to the back door, cracked it open, and peeked. Partially hidden by brush, his horse, Sunfish, stirred, but no other movement. No fresh tracks pocked the drifts.

William returned to the front door and waited. He counted to one hundred. He eased open the door and, in a crouch-walk, picked his way to the tree line. The snow was trampled by boot and shod hoof—and there was a red slash on the white. He bent closer; it was blood. The air hung quiet as a held breath. William was alone.

Jesse was alive, but wounded. It changed the odds— and the game.

William retrieved Sunfish and led the horse to the

crimson patch of snow. He followed a set of tracks from there but soon lost them as they intermingled with others going to and from the cabin.

Being too poor a tracker to trail Jesse, the only way William could catch him would be to guess his next move. How badly was the outlaw hurt? Still alive and able to ride, but probably needing a doctor.

Two doctors served the area: one in Lincoln and one at Fort Sumner. Jesse had friends in Lincoln. But would he return to the middle of the war if he were wounded? William put his money on Sumner.

Too bad, because though William could find his way back to Lincoln, he knew he would get lost cutting cross-country to the fort. William bowed to the necessity of returning to Lincoln.

Just a few hours left until sundown. William had nearly frozen to death the previous night before he found his way back to Jesse's cabin, and he feared wandering around in the dark and deadly cold. He would spend the night in the cabin and head back to Lincoln tomorrow.

Brilliant, cold stars replaced the sun. Another thought occurred to William as he stared at the diamond-flecked sky. Perhaps Jesse hadn't left the area. Perhaps he had been hiding, tending to his wound when William had ventured out to check the tree line. If Jesse had been only slightly wounded and in no immediate need of a sawbones, he might return to contest the cabin. Better than freezing.

On the other hand, if Jesse was gravely wounded, the cabin was his only chance for survival during the frigid night. He might even now be crawling his way here to fight desperately for its possession. More odds to consider.

William had no desire to stay up all night waiting for Jesse to make his move. If the outlaw lurked in the darkness, William needed to draw him in. He had to give him a target.

A dead man still lay in front of the cabin. William wanted to take the corpse back to Lincoln, but if left outside overnight, it would freeze to the ground. Dragging the body inside might entice Jesse into making a play and revealing himself.

William bent low and dashed to the corpse. He slung it over his shoulder, shielding his back, and humped it back to the cabin. Ten seconds that weighed like minutes.

No shot.

William slammed the door and dropped the body. He panted until he caught his breath. He searched through the window for movement.

A shape moved near a tree ten yards away.

William snapped his gun from his holster. The shape clarified. The dead man's horse foraged, seeking shelter under the tree.

No Jesse. Time for a bigger risk.

William sprinted back through the darkness to catch the dead man's horse. Keeping the animal between him and the trees, he walked it back to the cabin.

No shot.

William tied the horse up next to Sunfish. Confidence grew with every moment outside. He gave both horses some oats.

Once back inside, he made another pot of coffee. Maybe Jesse wasn't out there, but William figured the coffee was necessary to stay awake awhile. The warmth in the cabin and the hot brown liquid gave him an edge over a man, especially one waiting in the cold dark for an opportunity that dwindled with every passing moment.

After the moon rose and cast weak shadows across the open ground, William barred the door, shuttered the window, and risked sleep.

The next morning, refreshed and certain Jesse had left the area, William tied the dead man over the extra horse and climbed onto Sunfish. He led the burdened mount and returned to the grove where he and the Regulators had camped. Although deserted, there was enough of a trail for William to backtrack. Soon he found his bearings and picked his way through the wilderness toward Lincoln, dwarfed by the empty, snow-shrouded land through which he rode.

William reached Lincoln in late afternoon. He hitched Sunfish and the spare mount, still carrying its grisly burden, to the rail in front of Tunstall's store. Peering into every shadow, he stole down the street to Dr. Woods's office.

William took a deep breath and eased the door open. No sign of Jesse. He called for Dr. Woods.

The physician came out from his examination room. "William." Dr. Woods peered over his spectacles. "Are you hurt?"

"No. Jesse Evans and I fought. Dink, dink . . . I think he is wounded, and I wondered if he came here."

Dr. Woods shook his head. "I haven't seen him. Billy and that bunch came back yesterday with the bodies of Morton, Baker, Turner, and McCloskey." The doctor paused, eyes gone limpid. "I'm sorry. I know McCloskey was a friend of yours."

"I was there when Billy murdered him." William frowned. "I no longer ride with the Regulators."

Doctor Woods laid his hand on William's shoulder. "I was about to get some coffee at Wortley's. Join me?"

William smiled but shook his head. "I have to take c-c-care of Sunfish. And there's a d-d-dead man slung over a horse at Tunstall's."

The doctor sighed. "Best bring him here, then. I'll lay him out in the back with the others. I'm more undertaker than doctor today."

"There may be m-m-more to come."

The doctor glanced out the window, and the shadow of a frown crossed his face. "It's likely."

William followed his glance. Sheriff Brady and a deputy marched down the street toward the Tunstall store. "Brady was locked up when I rode out with the Regulators."

"His men let him out as soon as you all left. This is still his town."

"Locking him up was just symbolic anyway." William knew he had made an implacable enemy of the sheriff.

William moved toward the door. "That dead man slung across the horse is one of Jesse's men. I think Brady is going to want to t-t-talk to me. You stay here; I will b-b-bring the body to you when I am f-f-finished with Brady."

"Brady's just as likely to shoot you as talk to you. Why go looking for trouble?"

William stepped into the doorway but turned to Doctor Woods before going into the street. "Trouble is already here. It's him or me. I f-f-face it now or it comes looking for me, r-r-right into your office."

The Disappearance of Billy the Kid

Mindful the sun would soon set behind him and its glare hamper any shot Brady may fire at him, William followed a mere fifty feet behind the sheriff. He thought of drawing his gun but kept it holstered. If guns needed to speak, his would have first say either way.

Brady approached the horse with the body tied across it. The sheriff examined the corpse, lifting its head and staring into the lifeless face.

"It's Tom Hill," Brady said to his deputy. He crossed the street and then cocked the rifle he carried. Calling into the Tunstall store, he shouted, "Whoever killed this man, surrender yourself. Was it you, Billy?"

A fusillade erupted from the store.

In an instant the dark tornado took over, scattering William's thoughts like cattle in a lightning storm. Images flashed. Brady danced backward as bullet after bullet slammed into him. The startled deputy pulled at his holstered pistol, managing one wild shot before a round blew out the back of his head. He tumbled through a red spray.

The firing ceased and William gathered his thoughts. He was on the ground. Not wounded. Lawmen dead. Had he caused this violence by leaving the dead man Brady had called Tom Hill slung across his horse in front of the store?

Billy led four men from the store. The kid took note of William, then bent to retrieve Brady's rifle.

William rose to his feet. "Hoot. What ju—"

More shots sent William into a low crouch.

Billy cried out and grabbed his leg, cursing as a shot struck him.

Billy's men scattered, returning fire.

To William's right, crates stacked across the street from the Tunstall store provided shelter for the men firing at Billy. Sunfish and Tom Hill's horse neighed in terror, fighting their reins.

Billy struggled toward the Tunstall store.

William snap fired at the crates, forcing the gunmen hidden there to duck. With only moments to choose, he ran to Sunfish and loosened the reins. Part of him relaxed when Sunfish bolted up the street.

Billy still limped back toward the store, only three steps away from its shelter.

William drew the Remington and shot at the crates once more, buying a few more precious seconds. He barreled into Billy, grabbed him by the shoulders, and hauled him into the store.

The gunfire from the men behind the crates resumed moments later.

The hidden gunmen poured round after round into the building—shattering glass, splintering wood, and dancing the curtains. They were terrible marksmen; of the four Regulators who had gunned down Brady, thus far only Billy was wounded.

While the Regulators returned fire, William examined Billy's leg. Blood soaked the kid's pant leg in a steady stream. The bullet had gone through his lower thigh. William felt around the wound carefully, found both an entry and exit. The muscle was torn, but the bone was unbroken. Billy was lucky, though the bullet hole had to be cleaned and dressed or he risked death by infection.

Thinking ruefully of questions he wished he could ask Doc Woods, William searched for something to clean the wound. He found kerosene.

"When I was five, some farmer laid my back open with

a b-b-bullwhip." William picked up the can of kerosene, pried off the cap. "My father rubbed this stuff on. H-h-hurt like hell. He enjoyed it."

William called one of the other Regulators over and handed the man a rawhide braid. "Tie that around Billy's thigh as high up and as tight as you can. Then hold him d-d-down. Wretch, wretch."

William tore a strip of muslin from a skirt salvaged from the wreckage in the store. He soaked the absorbent material in kerosene, stirring it around with a thin ramrod from an old black powder pistol.

"Hurry up. My leg's going numb." Billy gritted his teeth.

"Numb is good," William said. "This is still going to h-h-hurt, but I will be as quick as I can."

Using the ramrod, William pushed the kerosene-soaked rag through the wound.

Billy writhed and his eyes nearly bulged from their sockets. Beads of sweat bathed his brow, and he clenched his teeth but did not cry out.

When satisfied the wound was clean, William wrapped it in linen torn from a petticoat pulled from a shelf. He loosened the tourniquet and signaled the restraining Regulator to relax.

Billy's labored breathing eased and he unclenched his jaw. He gave William a weak smile.

A lull in the gunfire allowed the men in the store to break out ammo and reload.

William's shoulders hitched in an involuntary shrug. If you had to hole up somewhere, there's no better place than a general store, he thought.

Though still ashen-faced, Billy interrupted William's thoughts. "Did you kill Jesse?"

"Wounded him, but he g-g-got away."

"So you're throwin' back in with us agin?" Billy groaned, clutching his wounded leg with both hands.

"Just sharing shelter."

A voice boomed from across the street. "You in the store. We want that murderin' son-of-a-bitch Billy. Send him out and we'll let the rest of you go."

"Not likely," shouted one of the Regulators.

"We had best g-g-get you out of here," William said, eyeing the back door. "Hoot." The corral, devoid of horses, provided no means of escape.

Billy tried to stand. He wobbled, wincing as he grabbed his leg. "I don't think I can walk. I sure as hell can't run."

The men across the street opened fire again. Tom Hill's horse pulled frantically at the reins in renewed panic.

"We need that horse," William said.

"There's no way," one of the defenders said. "It's no good to us in front of the store anyway. Now if it were out back, we could cover Billy while he took off."

"Offer a trade," Billy said. "Maybe they want some dry goods." He laughed, even while tears from pain pooled in the corners of his eyes.

Across the street the ambushers moved around, changing firing positions, looking for better angles.

One Regulator passed out rifles. "We can hold 'em off with these. Make your first shots count. Once they learn we've got rifles, they won't be so quick to show themselves."

William had an idea but had to act quickly. It was crucial the area behind the store remain clear. "One of you go out by the corral and m-m-make sure no one gets in behind us."

The man who had passed out the rifles took one in each hand and ducked out the back door.

"What do you have in mind?" Billy asked. "I still can't run."

"I have something even h-h-harder for you. Being quiet."

"How will I entertain myself?" Billy grunted when he moved his bandaged leg. "What's your plan?"

Glass shattered as a bullet from across the street smashed a lantern on a back shelf.

William opened the door to the private room where Alex and Emily had slept. "In here."

Billy grinned and shook his head. "You're counting pretty heavily on them respecting privacy, ain't ya?"

William grabbed a pry bar from a low shelf and entered the room. He walked to the bed and shoved it aside. "Give me a hand," he called to the Regulator who had helped him with Billy.

The Regulator stuck his head into the bedroom. "What do ya need?"

William set the pry bar between the boards on the floor where the bed had sat. "Pry up the floorboards. C-c-careful not to break any."

Nails groaned in protest as several boards popped loose. An earthen crawl space lay underneath the floor.

William dropped two blankets through the hole. "I think you should crawl in and lay d-d-down for a spell."

Billy looked in. "Reminds me of a grave." Grunting, he lowered himself in.

William replaced the loose boards and tapped the nails back into place. Resettling the bed over the spot returned the room to normal. With everything to his satisfaction, William left the room, shutting the door behind him. He looked out the back door and motioned to the guard there to return to the store.

"Did any of our friends from across the street snoop around b-b-back?"

"Nope." The guard looked around. "Hey, where's Billy?"

"He grabbed a horse from the corral and rode off." William stared into the guard's eyes.

The guard looked puzzled and raised a pointing finger as if about to speak; then his eyes went wide and his mouth snapped shut. A grin stole over his face. "Yeah, I get it."

"Gentlemen, it is t-t-time we surrendered. Invite those worthies across the street to come in and have a look." William walked to the front of the store and peered around the door frame.

"Billy's gone," he called across the street. "He went out the back while we k-k-kept you occupied."

"That's impossible," someone shouted. "He was shot—he didn't go nowhere."

"Just a graze. Hoot. We h-h-hoped you would think it bad enough so you were in no h-h-hurry to rush us. It bought Billy some t-t-time to make his getaway."

"And y'all fell for it," one of the other Regulators said. "We'll hold our fire; come look for yourselves."

Three men left cover and sidled warily over the icy street, glancing back to fellows still in hiding.

"What's to stop us from arresting the rest of you?" one of the approaching men asked.

William stepped forward. "M-m-me."

The three stopped, palms out chest high. "You promised you would hold your fire."

"While you satisfy yourself that Billy is g-g-gone." William pointed to the bodies of Brady and his deputy, and at Tom Hill, still tied across the saddle of the horse. "Then I expect you to take your dead and leave. Or j-j-join them. Your call."

The three men exchanged glances, and then the leader shrugged. "Okay. But if you're lying and Billy is still in there, we'll open up on you."

William laughed. "Hoot."

The Regulators stood aside while the three checked the store. One of them opened the door to the bedroom and glanced in. "Not here," he called to his fellows.

The man sounded relieved.

"Dad-burn it," the leader said. "The Kid got clean away." He glowcred at William, clenching his fists. Then, with an effort, he unclenched and pushed past William and back into the street.

One by one, like so many rabbits when the shadow of the hawk is gone, the men across the street popped out of their hiding places and milled about in the open. Two attended to Brady's body and two others to the slain deputy, grunting with the dead weight as they hoisted them like grain sacks—harvest from deadly seeds. The horse carrying Tom Hill's body plodded behind.

When the street cleared, William thought of Sunfish, who had bolted in that same direction. Rifles and ambush, he thought. Now that hostilities were in the open, this end of town was too dangerous. Wortley's, catty-corner from the House, was no longer safe. Even the McSweens', right next door, was threatened.

A squeak of the hinges on the rear exit made William turn, pistol snapping out. Susan McSween stood there, eyes wide.

"Hoot, sheet." William gasped and slid his gun back into its holster.

Susan eyed William and blew out a held breath. She walked through the store, shaking her head and frowning at the bullet holes and torn curtains. "All these ruined goods. Just look at the smashed china. It will take us a month—is that blood?"

She pointed to a red trail through the scattered dry goods. Her breath caught. "Who got hurt?"

"Billy," William said. "Shot in the leg. He is in Emily's r-r-room."

Her eyebrows drew together. "Those men left without him? Who convinced them to do that?" She gave William a long look.

William opened the door to the room and showed her Billy's hiding place. "Billy needs several d-d-days' rest before he can travel. B-b-best if his presence in the store is kept secret."

Susan bent to look under the bed. "Billy? Are you okay in there?"

"My leg's on fire and I'm thirsty," Billy said, his voice

muffled by the floorboards. "But I'm making new friends."

"Friends?"

"*Las cucarachas.* I told 'em I'd dance later." He laughed.

"I'll get you some water." Susan straightened up. "He can't stay down there, William."

William shrugged. "He needs to stay out of sight. But do what you l-l-like. I will be leaving soon."

"You leaving me again, William?" Billy asked when Susan left the room.

"I am going to hunt Jesse down. I think he is at Fort Sumner now, but probably not for long."

"If you wait for me to mend, I'll go with you."

"Two reasons why not. First, there is no t-t-time. Jesse could get p-p-patched up and slip away before I get there."

"Jesse wouldn't give me the slip." Billy's voice softly resonated from the crawl space. "I know his ways. Wait for me and I can help you track him."

"Still the other r-r-reason." William lost his balance and steadied himself on the bedstead. "I might be able to let you slip the halter on shooting Baker and Morton. There's a whole lot of killing been done, and more to c-c-come on both sides. War, not m-m-murder." William sighed and stood erect again. "But you were wrong to kill McCloskey. You made yourself a murdering outlaw, and those who r-r-ride with you will wear that b-b-brand as well."

A Sitting Duck

"People know this is a war," Billy said. "These range wars pop up all the time, and no one remains an outlaw when it's over, especially if they're on the winnin' side."

"Straight-up fights, but not m-m-murders. Murderers have to be hunted down or no one feels s-s-safe."

"That's ironic, comin' from you."

"I am always careful to live within the law. Those rules are b-b-brutal enough without taking extra liberties."

"You're a gunfighter."

"But not a m-m-murderer. There is an important difference, one that gets lost if I ride with you."

"I claim Baker and Morton were shot tryin' to escape and that McCloskey was killed helpin' 'em. Murder charges won't stick when this is all over."

"A lie, made up after the k-k-killing. Just like when Baker put a gun in Tunstall's hand and claimed self-defense."

"Not a lie. It's justice. They murdered Tunstall and lied, so I killed them and lied. Justice with a twist of sarcasm."

"Not sarcasm. Irony," William said.

"You wait and see. When this is over, there will be a new governor of the territory and the survivors of this war will be granted amnesty. So for now, no holds barred."

William sighed. "Maybe. Billy, we were friends once and I hope for your s-s-sake it will be as you say. But I am riding alone."

William left the small bedroom and glanced out the back door to the corral. In the fading light of dusk, he saw Sunfish eating hay from the rick. "So you found your way back." William straightened his gun belts. "Time to go."

The door opened and Susan brought in a tray of hot food. The aroma of beef stew wafted through the store. William amended his plan. First thing in the morning.

After a feast on Susan's stew, William strode to the Torreón, an old watchtower he used as sleeping quarters when in Lincoln. He stretched out in the beehive-shaped mud-and-brick two-story structure. He hoped Jesse might come to Lincoln after all. It would save a trip to Fort Sumner. If so, this tower made an ideal fortified position.

On an impulse, he buried a box of ammunition in the beaten earth floor.

The next morning William went to the McSweens' for breakfast. Because they shared his fears that it was no longer safe to eat at Wortley's, they provided food in their home to whoever among their friends was in town.

The rising sun threw crisp shadows across the veranda. William squinted at Susan as she served him. "Has Emily left for England? Or is she still in Fort Sumner?" William squashed down on the sudden hope that flared at the thought.

"I put her on the stage to Fort Worth myself. From there she'll go by train to New York and then sail home."

"She had enough m-m-money for the trip?"

"I advanced her some, and her father will wire more to her in New York. I would have felt better if I could have gone at least as far as Fort Worth with her, but things here needed tending."

The sunshine seemed duller to William now that Emily was really gone. "What do you intend to d-d-do about the store?"

"Alex will run it. This fight isn't over, William."

"And John's ranch?"

Susan shook her head and her shoulders slumped. "Abandoned for now. Emily gave it to me, told me she had no use for anything out here in the American West.

I'll hold on to it, but after what happened to John, it's too dangerous to keep it running. The ranch is so far out of town, and there're not enough men to guard both it and the store."

"I would stay to help, but I doubt Jesse is coming to me and I have lost enough time." William reached into an inner pocket of his vest, drew out five gold coins, and gave them to Susan. "I hope Alex can k-k-keep the store going."

Susan's eyebrows raised. "What are these for?"

"I made free with the g-g-goods at the store. This should c-c-cover it."

"This is too much money." Susan tried to return three of the coins.

"Keep it. There might be h-h-hard times ahead."

She clasped his hand. "You will always be welcome here."

After eating his tortillas and beans, William offered to take some food to Billy before leaving for Fort Sumner.

Although William did not think the Tunstall store was watched by Dolan's men when it was closed, he took the breakfast in through the back door just in case. The bedroom was locked, the key hanging on a hook on the wall. He knocked on the door three times, then unlocked and opened it. He winced when he noted the bed had been pushed to the side of Billy's hiding place.

"Hope no one comes in for a s-s-surprise inspection," he said, pulling a board away to hand the food down to Billy.

"Door's kept locked." Billy's voice echoed from beneath the floorboards. "No one is gonna walk in on me by surprise."

"How is the leg today?"

"Itches. Did you really have to ram that kerosene rag through me like that?" Billy lay on his back and looked at William through the narrow opening left by the missing board.

"Itching is good. Means the wound is h-h-healing."

"Do you still mean to chase off after Jesse?" Billy took a bite of his tortilla-wrapped beans.

William nodded. "I wanted to bring you some victuals f-f-first. I will be riding out in a minute."

Billy chewed over the idea along with the mouthful of food. He swallowed. "Jesse is pretty good with a rifle."

"Did not do him much good at our last meeting." William shook his head, discarding the disturbing thought that he might have just been lucky. He didn't want his thoughts to ride down that trail.

"Just telling you so you'll be careful. You might want to think about taking a rifle too."

"I will, though I am not that g-g-good with one."

"Another thing: Jesse and his gang used to hang out

down in Las Cruces, but there was a couple of killings so I don't know if he'll head that way. He has family in Missouri and Texas, so he might light out to those places if things get too hot for him in New Mexico."

"I will keep that in mind." William stood. "So long, Billy."

"If none of that gives you reason enough to wait for me, then you're a fool."

"Hoot. Been called worse."

William left the bedroom and picked a Winchester '73 from the Tunstall stock. As it shot rapidly and accurately, it had a reputation as the common man's equalizer against all the varmints that had to be cleared out before the land was civilized.

William knew himself to be no common man, and wondered if that made him a varmint. Well, Jesse had a rifle, and he was a varmint for sure.

He left a note for Susan:

Helped myself to one of the Winchesters and a box of bullets. You can reach me through the marshal in Fort Sumner.

—William

He packed his gear onto Sunfish and left Lincoln.

*   *   *

The afternoon sun cast long shadows as William arrived at Fort Sumner. Cattle pens, nearly devoid of winter beeves stocked for the reservation, gave the town a lonely feel. The little church where they had buried John Tunstall brooded at the end of the street. William turned his eyes away from it to stem a tide of sad memories.

He hitched Sunfish to the rail in front of the marshal's office. He entered to find McAdams locking the door to the cells in the back.

"Thought you should know I am b-b-back," William said.

McAdams studied him closely. "Any particular business bring you here?"

"I am looking for Jesse Evans. I thought he might need to see the doctor."

McAdams walked around to sit behind his desk. "The doctor already saw Jesse. Now I've got him locked up."

"Here?" William's gaze flew to the locked door of the cell block.

"Turns out I had an old warrant for Jesse's arrest for stealing reservation beef."

"May I see him?"

McAdams held out a hand, palm up. "Let me have your guns first."

William laughed. "Are you afraid he will try to t-t-take them from me?"

McAdams held William's gaze and did not smile. "I heard what Billy did to Morton and Baker. No prisoner will be murdered while in my custody."

"I am not like that." William handed over his guns. "I l-l-left Billy and the Regulators. I ride alone."

"Maybe so. But I'm not taking any chances." McAdams laid William's revolvers on top of the desk. "They'll be waiting right here for you when you're finished."

McAdams rose from his chair and pulled at a ring of keys on his belt. He preceded William to a heavy wooden door with a rectangle of bars at head height. Fetid air drafted through the opening. McAdams stabbed a key into the lock, iron scraping against iron, and turned the key to the solid *thunk* of metal. Hinges groaned as he pulled the door open.

William stepped past the marshal and into a corridor between the wall on his left and four iron cages on his right. The only light that filtered in came through high barred windows, one at the end of the hall and one in each cell.

There was one prisoner. He lay on a narrow bunk in the second cage, holding one hand behind his head and staring at the ceiling. His shirt was open and a bandage wrapped his torso. A stain of blood, sharp-edged and round, broke the white even field of the wrapping below the man's right ribs. The man's face remained shadowed.

William moved to the front of the cell door. "You are the only one l-l-left, Jesse."

Jesse swung his feet off the bunk and brought his face into the sunlight. His jaw clenched. "I've still got a loyal gang."

William held up a hand and counted on his fingers. "Baker, Morton, and Hill are d-d-dead. You are the only one left."

"D-d-dead," Jesse said, mimicking William's flopping, head-twisting motion. "So what? I've got other help."

William willed himself to stillness. He pointed at the red blossom below Jesse's ribs. "I killed Hill. And I almost g-g-got you."

Jesse shrugged and then winced. "Just lost a bit of bark. I've been hurt worse stealin' sheep."

"The marshal says he has you on a r-r-rustling charge," William said. "They hang rustlers, do they not?" He drew a steadying breath, steeling himself not to spasm. "Dead is dead."

"They won't hang me. In a way I've got you to thank for that. Doc says it'll be several days before I'm recovered. I'll be out of here by then."

"I hope so," William said. "I do not want you to h-h-hang for rustling. I want to kill you myself."

"Suits me. I've been thinking about facing you ever since Wichita."

A Conversation

Jesse swung his feet off the cot and sat up. "I could have killed you at the cabin. When you got in that lucky shot, it scared and hurt me, but I knew I wasn't gonna die. I could have waited for you to come and put a bullet through your heart."

William shrugged, lost his balance, and grasped the bars for support. "Am I supposed to thank you?"

Jesse shook his head. "I'm not ready to kill you, yet. You fascinate me."

"You put me on the trail of being a g-g-gunfighter. I want to kill you just for that."

"If I did, I'm proud of it. I like you." Jesse stood and grasped the cell bars, bringing his face close to William's. "Did you help Billy murder Morton and Baker?"

"I was there," William said, holding Jesse's stare. "I did not shoot either one."

"You didn't stop him either. So Sheriff Brady will arrest you too. Maybe even send the warrant to McAdams to do it. Imagine, we could be cellmates." Jesse paused, looked around his cell, spit. "Being locked up is worse than death."

"You must not have heard the n-n-news. Brady is dead." He read shock, then doubt in Jesse's eyes. "Billy did it. And I d-d-did not stop him then either."

"You were there?"

"I was. I did not fire at Brady, but I gladly h-h-helped Billy escape."

"So you're an accomplice." Jesse took a half step back from the bars. "Just as bad."

William's shoulder hitched upward in a semblance of a shrug. "The way I see it, Brady had broken jail."

"What?" Jesse's face puckered in scorn.

"Brady was locked up on a w-w-warrant issued by Marshal McAdams and certified by the t-t-town constable. But his men let him out and he went gunning for Billy."

Jesse broke eye contact and stared into a corner of the cell. After a minute of thought, he said, "And now you're here to kill me."

"Yes, b-b-but not while you are unarmed and locked in a cage."

"You shot from ambush at the cabin. Not that much of a difference."

The thought sobered him. At the time it seemed acceptable, but now looking back, he wondered. Was he on the trail to becoming a murderer? "Hoot." The involuntary noise and lurch against the cell bars snapped his reverie.

He shot a look at Jesse's face. The man's eyes were arresting; was it calculation or understanding moving in their depths?

"The man at the cabin was armed, and you are not. I have not sunk so l-l-low as to shoot an unarmed man. Hoot. That would be murder."

"Billy is loose, and he won't be as meticulous about it."

"Met-ic-u-lus?" He frowned at the unfamiliar word.

"It means careful, paying attention to details." Jesse grinned. "What I mean is Billy won't bother with little things like the law when he comes. He'll just shoot between the bars."

"The marshal will not let him b-b-back here with his guns; you are safe in your cage."

Jesse glanced at the barred window of his cell. "Billy's an outlaw and doesn't give a damn about the law."

"Billy might be an outlaw, b-b-but you are the one locked up."

"Ha! Compared to you and Billy, I'm the only free man."

He stared at Jesse, unsure of what the man meant. But he did not want to give the murderer the satisfaction of asking.

"I'm the only one with a choice," Jesse said. "I traveled with Billy and know that he can't control his impulses. Now loyalty to a dead man drives him. Anger, insult, insecurity. He can be ridden like a horse if you pull the reins right."

"Billy is his own man." William smiled. "Mostly he is fun to be around."

"Probably because he saw you as some sort of pet," Jesse said. "You don't ride with him now, though. Why not?"

Because he acts on impulse, William thought. Jesse was right, and the pet comment made an angry suspicion boil around in his gut. He refused to give Jesse the satisfaction of admitting it. "Because he is a murderer and I am not. Hoot. Our trails parted."

"So you left your friends and set off alone after me," Jesse said, shaking his head. "I'm sure you could have waited and had help tracking me. Why didn't you?"

"I did not want to."

"An emotional choice. See, you're not free either. You're as driven as Billy."

"Nothing has a s-s-saddle on me."

"Your sickness does, clown. Your illness carries you along like some big stage coach; you're just along for the ride."

"I am what I am." William rested his thumbs on his empty holsters. "I have no choice in the matter, emotional or otherwise."

"So you choose to tell yourself."

He shook his head in disgust. Talking to Jesse left him more than unsatisfied; it disturbed him as well, like Jesse was trying to throw a lasso around William's thoughts. "All this talk will not do you any g-g-good. You murdered my friend, and I will see that you pay for it."

Jesse smiled and lay back down on his bunk. "Been nice talkin' to ya."

6

Trying to Free Jesse

William left the cell block and retrieved his guns from McAdams's desk. He took Sunfish to the stable, then sought his own dinner at a café. Steak and beans.

His thoughts spun as he stirred the sweet sauce through the beans. Jesse was caught, but William couldn't take the next step, couldn't shoot an unarmed man. Locked in a cell, Jesse wouldn't be armed any time soon. Maybe never again. Perhaps a judge might set Jesse free. Or perhaps he might escape.

He had no choice but to hang around Fort Sumner, hoping for something to develop. Waiting, not acting, reminded him of what Jesse had said; he was not making choices—not the true choices, not the ones that mattered.

William stabbed at his steak. He could leave, forswearing

his vengeance, or he could toss Jesse a gun through the barred window. But McAdams would still have to unlock the cell, and probably get killed for his trouble. William would not risk that.

Suppose he tossed both gun and keys into the cell—then ambushed Jesse when he ran from the jail? Was that a better choice than doing nothing? It didn't feel that way. He thought of McAdams still in harm's way, and himself turned outlaw for aiding Jesse's escape.

Frustrated, William chewed on his steak, tougher meat than he liked.

*   *   *

The next day he asked McAdams, "What is going to h-h-happen to Jesse now? Will he be tried on that beef-stealing charge?"

"Eventually. First we have to round up the witnesses, if we can find 'em, and then send for the circuit judge. Not sure it's worth all that trouble; the charge is for theft, not rustling. Time we get it all done, he'd probably be let go for time served. I'm just using the charge to hold him—keep the Dolan gang off balance."

"Suppose you let him go now? Tell me first, of course."

McAdams eyed William with quiet intensity. "You wouldn't be asking me to participate in a murder?"

"Not at all. You let Jesse go, g-g-give him his gun, and tell him I am waiting for him in the street."

"I would need some legal reason to do that." McAdams rubbed his chin. "Like if the charges were dropped."

"Who f-f-filed the charges?"

"The Indian Bureau. Jesse's accused of stealing beef designated for the reservation."

William's head twitched and his left cheek touched his shoulder. "Don't you represent the government here?"

"Only as a marshal. Once a charge's been filed it isn't up to me to drop it. That's a judge's decision."

"Last week, after Tunstall's funeral, you issued us warrants for Brady and his gang. Can you not play judge again, one m-m-more time?"

McAdams leaned back in his chair and blew out a deep breath. "Knowing why you want me to release Jesse—not this time."

"Is what I want so far outside the law? I ask only for a chance to fight Jesse fairly. It would have happened already if you did not have him locked up."

"The beef he stole was the property of the army. If you get Colonel Dudley, the fort commander, to drop the charges, then I would have to release Jesse."

"I recall that you claimed the fort commander was part of the Santa Fe Ring with Dolan and the governor." He tapped McAdams's desk three times. "Why has the colonel not tried to get Jesse released?"

McAdams snapped his fingers. "Maybe it hasn't come to his attention that I have Jesse."

William cocked an eye at McAdams. "Ask him if he wants to pursue the charge."

"So you can gun Jesse down?" McAdams shook his head in doubt. "Doesn't feel right."

"Tell the colonel the truth; the trial is a lot of trouble for l-l-little result. If he agrees to drop the charges, you give Jesse back his guns and let him go."

McAdams frowned, shook his head.

"I will give Jesse a chance. More than he might otherwise get. Remember, Billy is on the loose."

7

A New Plan

"We'll deal with the charges later," McAdams said. "Jesse's been wounded, and I won't release him until the doc says he's okay."

"When will that be?"

"A couple of days at least."

William turned to leave. "I will have a t-t-talk with the doctor and Colonel Dudley."

"You might think twice about going onto the military post. Dudley is lord and master and no friend of yours."

"Do you intend to ask h-h-him to drop the charge against Jesse?"

"Not now, but I'll talk to him about it when Jesse has healed a bit more." McAdams sighed and rubbed his forehead. "You ought to do the same. If Dudley and Jesse are in cahoots, and you ask for Jesse's release, the colonel might put two and two together and opt to keep him in jail."

"Unless he thinks Jesse can t-t-take me."

"I don't know, William. Your reputation says he can't."

An inkling of a plan took form in William's mind. "How does Colonel Dudley f-f-feel about gambling?"

McAdams didn't answer, though his brow furrowed in thought.

Smiling, William left the marshal's office.

The Fort Sumner military surgeon also served as the town doctor. So, in spite of McAdams's warnings about venturing onto the military compound, William had to go. The hair tickle of his tongue reminded him that he entered enemy territory.

The gates of the wood-and-adobe fort stood open with weeds and dirt accumulated beneath the stoop timbers; a dusty spiderweb hung from a hinge. The sentries stood relaxed at their posts, favoring him with only a glance. The fort smelled of manure and bacon.

Soldiers passed to and fro across the parade ground of packed earth at the center of the fort. Adobe buildings bordered this rectangle on three sides. William asked a passing trooper where he could find the doctor. The soldier waved his hand in the general direction of the row of buildings to William's left. Horses neighed on his right.

He ambled down the boardwalk until he saw a sign stenciled in black letters on a whitewashed board: ALBERT STONE MD MAJOR USARMY. He knocked and entered.

The small room had five empty chairs and a desk spread with papers. A man wearing four stripes on his sleeve sat at the desk reading a penny dreadful. He looked up. "Sir?"

"May I t-t-talk to the doctor?" William tottered as he spoke.

The sergeant sat straighter in his chair. "Are you injured? Maybe you should sit down."

"I am fine. I just need to ask the d-d-doctor a question about one of his patients."

The sergeant stood. "Take a seat." He motioned to the row of empty chairs. "I'll get the doctor." He disappeared through an inner doorway.

William moved to a chair and had just settled when a gray-haired man, face furrowed by age lines around a pockmarked nose, emerged through that same inner doorway. A major's gold leaf clung to the epaulettes of his rumpled uniform.

"I'm Doctor Stone. How can I help you?" The man's voice was firmer than the flesh that produced it.

William staggered to his feet and grabbed the wall for support. "Hoot."

"Hoot?" Doctor Stone's eyes flashed over William's body in quick appraisal. "Come back to my examination room."

"I am fine," William said but followed the doctor.

"Sit on the table, please." The doctor pointed at an elevated bench in the center of the room, then pulled tarnished instruments from a cupboard. He fastened a reflector around his brow with a leather strap and picked up a stethoscope. "Open your shirt."

William sat, but crossed his arms over his chest. "I am not here for me. I want to know how Jesse Evans is doing."

"Is Mr. Evans a friend of yours?" The doctor put the ear pieces of the stethoscope in his ears and waved the bell-shaped end about, trying to place it on William's chest. "Open your shirt, please."

William grasped the doctor's hand. "I am the one who shot him."

Doctor Stone pulled the stethoscope from his ear and refocused onto William's face. "Some kind of accident? What do you want?"

"I want to know when Jesse will be well enough"—William grimaced and his neck torqued to the left—"to be r-r-released from jail."

Doctor Stone eyed William's movements. "How long have you had this affliction?"

"I will answer your question; then you answer mine. I have had this 'affliction' as long as I can remember."

"Ever have blackouts or seizures?"

William shook his head. "Now, my turn. How about Jesse?"

"It was touch and go at first, but he is healing." Doctor Stone put his thumb at the side of William's left eye and rolled the lower lid down. He leaned in for a close look. A flash from the reflector dazzled William.

William grunted, certain the doctor had exaggerated Jesse's injury. Only four days since the gunfight and Jesse appeared in too good a shape for someone described as 'touch and go.' "So he is well enough to be r-re-released, then?"

"I want to keep him for observation for at least a week. Your shot broke a couple of ribs. Caused a slow internal bleed. Thank God the bleeding stopped and there was no infection. If your bullet had hit a fraction to the left. Well . . ." The doctor pulled his face back from scrutinizing William's eyes. "Does anyone else in your family have your condition?"

"J-j-just me," William said. "So you are only holding Jesse for observation? There is nothing wrong with him?"

"Nothing wrong?" Doctor Stone scowled. "You nearly shot him in the liver. During the war I saw plenty of similar wounds. We called them the one-day death. Of course, those were minié balls—did a lot more collateral damage than your .45. Now, if you'd been using one of those front loaders, Mr. Evans would be stone dead now, and a miserable day he would have had dying."

"Lucky for him this is the 1870s, then." William pushed lightly against the doctor's chest. "Jesse is right-handed—is he able to use a gun?"

Stone shrugged and took William's hand in both of his. He pushed and pulled, feeling the bones of hand and wrist, working his way up toward the elbow. "Are you able to stop the tics and tremors on your own? Like if you concentrate really hard?"

"Sometimes, but not for long. The only time they go away completely is when I am, hoot, p-p-pre-occupied."

"You do seem to have a bit of a stubborn streak in you," Doctor Stone said. "Single-minded, I might say."

William smiled. "Back to Jesse. Can he use a gun?"

"You mean like engage in a gunfight?" The doctor frowned. "There's nothing wrong with his nerves, nor his eyes. If he could shoot before, he still can."

William took a steadying breath. "Doctor, Jesse is a gunfighter. Can he still draw his gun and fire as fast and true as he did before I shot him?"

"What? Today?" Doctor Stone looked as though he would laugh. "His right side is stitched and bandaged, his torso wrapped, and his muscles sore as hell. So no, not today, but some day? Sure, I don't see why not." The doctor lowered his voice. "Don't worry. You have plenty of time to get out of town."

"Jesse and I have unfinished business. He set me up as

a gunfighter. He killed my friend and tried to kill me. I will not wait for him to try again at a time of his choosing."

"You're a gunfighter?" Doctor Stone scratched his temple. "You must be joking."

William shook his head. He had no more questions.

Doctor Stone finished his examination. He rubbed his chin and gazed into the distance. "Puzzling case," he said quietly. Then he spoke more directly to William: "I'm not certain yet. Maybe some nerve tonics will help. Let me look into it. Come see me again next week."

William sighed. "Doctor, I did not come to you for treatment. I want to finish my business with Jesse and be on my way."

"I can't promise anything, but maybe there is something that will help your condition. Wouldn't you like to stop the twitching and get control of your body?"

William shook his head as he stood up. "No other doctor ever thought there was a chance of that." He walked out of the office and onto the boardwalk that ran along the edge of the parade ground.

Something to stop his twitching? If the tonic took away his speed as well as his twitches, he'd be dead within an hour.

An Invitation to a Gunfight

William stood in front of the doctor's office and looked to his left at the headquarters building. The two-story edifice of brick and wood dominated the parade field.

He wanted to propose something to Colonel Dudley in such a way as to let the commander put his own brand on the idea. Some entertainment for the troops: a gunfight between William and Jesse with the colonel controlling the betting sure to take place. For the idea to work, Jesse must have a fair chance.

But, since Jesse would not be ready for at least another week, today was too soon to involve Dudley. "Hoot."

Laughter broke William's reverie. Several troops ringed around him, their faces reflecting a mix of surprise, curiosity, and disdain.

One beefy man wearing corporal stripes spit in the dirt. "What in the hell are you doing here?"

"I just finished with the d-d-doctor," William said.

"The doctor, huh?" The corporal sneered. "What's wrong with you anyway? Is it catching?"

"No." William made to push between two of the troopers but missed his footing when he stepped off the boardwalk. He widened his stance to regain his balance, but a rough shove knocked him down.

The soldiers laughed.

Palms scraped and ears burning, he pushed to his feet and dusted himself off. He remembered he was on a military post and surrounded by troops. Armed troops. He faced his tormentors, catching sight of the fort's gate as he did. A long way off.

"Are you sure you ain't just drunk?" one of the troopers asked. "You look drunk to me."

The man wore a sidearm in a boxy military holster. The flap was closed. William looked around; all the flaps were closed.

"I am not drunk. Have none of you nothing b-b-better to do than to stand around g-g-gawking?"

The beefy corporal pointed at William's belt. "Hey, look, the man's carrying guns. He can't stand up, but he's wearing two guns."

"Careful, O'Rourke. He could be a real dangerous

man," laughed a trooper.

"Yeah, he's probably a gunfighter," said another trooper, and they all laughed louder than before.

"I am."

Another round of laughter, louder still. A few more troops drifted over.

William waited, a smile playing across his mouth, for the laughter to stop.

"You couldn't shoot the hat off my head, standing right next to me," the corporal said.

"No. I would shoot your h-h-head off your shoulders."

The corporal scowled. "Watch out, or you'll talk yourself into some real trouble." He puffed out his chest. "Take off your guns."

"I have no r-r-reason to take them off."

The corporal's eyes went wide, and his face turned the color of raw liver. "Take 'em off."

The troopers tensed.

William backed up three steps and faced the man squarely. "Anyone think this fat t-t-tub of lard can take me, put up some m-m-money."

The soldier went for his gun, his fumbling draw ruined when he couldn't get the flap open.

There was no danger from the fool so the dark tornado did not descend. William drew his revolver with a quiet dignity and pointed it at the man's heart.

"If this had been a real gunfight, Corporal, you would be d-d-dead. You should be careful who you try to p-p-push around." He returned his revolver to his holster in a smooth, unhurried motion.

A wasp-buzz of conversation started among the gathered troops. None would meet his gaze.

He had an idea, one he would turn loose to see who roped and branded it. "There is not one of you h-h-here who can match me. Unlike like the man Colonel Dudley has l-l-locked in the marshal's office."

He turned to go, and a shaky voice shouted after him. "Who's the colonel got locked up?"

Careful to hide his smile, William called over his shoulder, "An outlaw named Jesse Evans."

Stable Advice

Having decided to stay at Fort Sumner, William looked for work at the stable, where his tab for Sunfish totaled over a dollar.

"About what I have left," William told the stableman, showing him the coin. Then a sudden twitch almost sent the coin flying from his hand. He grimaced, willing his arms to be still. He took a steadying breath. "How about I work off my debt instead? Maybe let me s-s-sleep here too?"

The stableman squinted. "You sure you're safe around a pitchfork?"

William smiled at the same old question. "I am sure."

The stableman put his hands on the small of his back and stretched. He looked at the manure-covered floor, the row of stalls, and a large haystack inside the rear door of the stable. "Can't pay you nothin' but room and board."

"That is all I need," William said, shaking the man's hand. "Thanks."

"Okay, get to work, but leave the currying to me." The stableman picked up a couple of brushes and disappeared into a stall.

William tied a bandana over his mouth and nose and started pitching hay. The rhythmic work made his tics and flopping lunges less frequent. Mindless work—it let him relax. He thought about Doctor Stone's idea; nerve tonics might get him full control over his body. Did he really want that? What if it changed him in other ways? Perhaps Jesse had been right and he was afraid to get off the "stagecoach."

In the early afternoon, William unloaded feed sacks from a wagon beside the stable. He glanced up and saw a black surrey hitched in front of the marshal's office. Gold lettering on the side proclaimed NEW MEXICO TERRITORIAL GOVERNOR'S OFFICE.

He smelled manure in the air, and it wasn't from the stable.

William finished unloading and stacking the feed sacks and asked Emmett, the stableman, for a work break.

"Sure, you been working hard all afternoon." Emmett eyed the stacked feed. "Come back at supper time and help me feed the horses after we eat."

"Thank you." He tucked his sweat-soaked bandana into a pant pocket. A jerk of his torso caused him to bump into the side of a stall. He straightened and turned to Emmett. "Supper at s-s-six?"

Emmett nodded and rubbed his forehead. "You make me nervous when you do stuff like that. I don't see how you manage to not hurt yourself."

"Years of practice. See you at six."

William adjusted his guns and strode out of the stable. When he turned toward the marshal's office, he saw that the one-horse surrey was gone.

As a caution, he used the boardwalk instead of walking in the center of the street. When he reached the marshal's office, he stood listening at the door for a moment.

Someone moved inside so William pushed the door open.

McAdams looked up from behind his desk, first at William and then at the clock on the wall. "William?"

"I saw a buggy from the g-g-governor's office tied up in front. I thought you might need some help, the governor being a crook and all."

"I could use some help all right, but not the kind you mean." McAdams sighed. "Governor Axtell got wind of that mess over in Lincoln. He invalidated those writs I gave you, so nothing that the Regulators did there—the arrests of Brady, Morton, and Baker—is legal. That means the Regulators acted outside the law, and the governor has declared them all criminals."

"What about Jesse? Did he get released?"

McAdams shook his head. "That's still an army matter. But I'm sure that Colonel Dudley will do whatever the governor says. I'll probably get orders for his release"—the marshal took a deep breath—"tomorrow."

"Will you release him then?" William asked. "No matter what Doctor Stone says?"

"If his release is officially ordered, I'll have to. I can't legally hold him."

"Sounds like the governor just did me a f-f-favor," William said, though he wondered if Jesse would be able to handle a gun so soon. He would have to force Jesse to draw first. It wouldn't feel so much like murder if Jesse did.

"Will you give Jesse back his guns when you release him?"

"I'll have to, but I'll suggest he not wear them until he's out of town."

William pulled a chair away from its resting spot by the wall and sat down. "I will wait here."

McAdams stood. "Don't. You're on the wrong side of the law now, William. You shoot Jesse and your name will be on a wanted poster within a day."

"Not if it is s-s-self-defense."

"You don't understand the situation. It won't matter. The governor will put a price on your head."

"I will have an army of w-w-witnesses." William's mood lightened as he said it. But he knew there was much to be done to make it true.

McAdams glared at him.

William rose from his chair. "Okay, waiting here is a b-b-bad idea. I have some things to do before Jesse's release."

Everything was happening too quickly, William thought as he walked back to the stable. Not enough time for Jesse to heal properly. Too soon for a showdown to be set up between them by gambling soldiers. Three days more and he could have finished with Jesse.

William took a cold supper with Emmett at the stable.

"You look like you got a team of horses running around in your head," Emmett said as they ate. "Whatja thinking about?"

"Unfinished business," William said. "I am thinking about how to f-f-finish it."

"Don't know what business you're talking about, but I've always found the best way is to go right at it. You can't get a horse to shoe itself. Somebody's got to knock in the nails."

"That is what I like about working in a stable. Choices are clear and simple, with no m-m-moral implications."

Emmett snorted. "You're right on that score. No use talking morals with your mount. You saddle up and ride off. Whether to good or bad, no one blames the horse."

"My business is with a man, and there is p-p-plenty of blame already."

"Then let the law handle it."

"The law is to blame for m-m-most of it. How do I set it right and still stay within the l-l-law, when the law itself is corrupt?"

"Which law are you trying to stay within? Man's law or God's law?" Emmett took a bite of ham.

"Both. At least the p-p-parts that are not corrupt."

Emmett swallowed and shrugged. "I'm pretty good with knots. Pulling on 'em just makes 'em worse. You got to find the slip point and ease it." He yawned. "Sleep on it. Maybe things will look clearer in the morning."

William sighed and scraped his supper leavings into the stable yard. He fed the horses and then currycombed his own. When finished, he hand-fed some oats to Sunfish and stroked the horse's neck. "So what do you think I should do?" He laughed.

Sunfish blinked his green eye.

Stacking the Deck

The next morning William shoveled feed into the ricks for the horses. He wondered if one of the stabled animals belonged to Jesse. He had not seen Jesse's mount that day at the cabin, but he did recall the trail of prints that confounded his own tracking skills. He needed to know which horse Jesse rode.

When he finished feeding the animals, he picked up a file from Emmett's blacksmithing tools and slipped it into the back pocket of his pants.

Interrupting Emmett as he was combing one of the other horses, William asked, "Do you know who Jesse Evans is?"

"That outlaw the marshal has locked up," Emmett said. "Is he your unfinished business?"

"Does one of these h-h-horses belong to him?"

Emmett squinted along the row of stalls and pointed to one. "Don't know if he owns her, but he rode in on that sorrel mare."

The horse nickered and shook her head.

"What happens to the horse if Jesse does not return?"

"I'll sell her to pay off his debts."

"How is his bill standing now?"

Emmett rubbed his chin. "He owes me for three days. Can't say about other places around town, but I doubt it's much, seeing as he's been locked up and eating off the government and all."

"I think he will be short. But if not, s-s-stall him." He hitched at his gun belt.

Emmett shrugged. "Well, we'll see."

William picked up an armload of straw and carried it to the stall that held Jesse's horse. He did not expect Emmett would delay Jesse's departure if it came to that. He had what he wanted; he knew which horse belonged to Jesse.

William spread the fresh straw in the stall and lifted the left forefoot of the sorrel mare in a blacksmith's grip. With the file he cut the letter *J* into the horse's shoe. He filed an *E* on the right shoe.

Later, William helped Emmett handle a late morning arrival. The horse was a mare coming into season, so William penned her in a separate corral behind the stable. When this chore was finished to Emmett's satisfaction, William took a break from his labors and walked to the marshal's office.

McAdams sat eating a plateful of corn and beans at his desk. He looked up when William entered the office and tapped the plate with his fork. "Want some?"

William shook his head. "How is Jesse today?"

"Same as before. Doctor Stone was in to see him earlier. Says it'll still be a couple of days before the bandages can come off."

"Who is paying Doctor Stone's b-b-bill? Did Jesse have any money when you arrested him?"

"The doctor hasn't said anything about a bill, but I guess the territory'll pay it." McAdams pulled open a desk drawer and sorted through its contents. "Jesse had nine dollars and thirty-three cents when I arrested him."

William leaned over the desk. "When you are forced to release Jesse, can you hold his money back?"

"For what reason?"

"Tell him you put it in the bank for safekeeping and have to withdraw it." He rocked on his feet and grabbed the desk for support. "Just something to keep him in town for an extra day or two."

McAdams rolled his eyes and crooked a smile. "I don't think so." He pushed the drawer closed.

William stared at McAdams. "If Billy had not shot

Baker and Morton, would you be making all this fuss about releasing Jesse while I am around?"

"Probably not. But then your friend Billy brought murder into the play."

"Jesse is a killer. Why are you protecting him?"

"Jesse is in the hands of the law, and he will answer to the law for what he has done. To the law, William, not to vigilante justice."

"You signed those arrest warrants after Tunstall's funeral. You were willing to turn Jesse and his men over to vigilantes then."

"I was willing to shade the law a bit to keep things even. But those were arrest warrants, not licenses to kill. I can't shade murder."

"Not murder. I am going to k-k-kill him in a fair fight."

McAdams slowly pushed back his chair and stood. "Look, William, I like you. If you run into Jesse somewhere and shoot it out, I hope you win. But as long as he's in my custody, setting up a gunfight is too close to condoning the killing. The law can't do that."

William rapped his knuckles on the marshal's desk. "Hoot."

"I don't expect that Jesse will be in my custody much longer," McAdams said. "If you catch and kill him outside of town, well, it would serve him right for pulling strings with the governor. But I can have no hand in it."

"Will you hold him at least until the Doc says he is fit?"

"I'm in no hurry to release him. But when the writ comes, I have to let him go."

"Has Colonel Dudley been to see you?" William asked.

"No. I don't understand it. I expected to hear from him by last evening."

He didn't understand the delay either but felt glad of it. When Jesse was released, William would have a chance to track him out of town. He hoped Jesse would be well enough for a fair fight, or at least what others would call a fair fight: both men armed and drawing on each other. With his faster draw, that's as fair as any of his gunfights got.

He shrugged. It was what it was.

Satisfied that he had done all he could through the marshal, he left the office and started back to the stable.

Led by a third man with sergeant's stripes, two soldiers with shouldered rifles marched toward him. Their stern countenances suggested official business.

A chill ran along William's spine and his thoughts swirled. Was this Jesse's release?

He stopped to watch, expecting to fall in behind the soldiers and trail them to McAdams's office. But the sergeant veered aside and marched straight to William, flanked by armed troopers.

"Colonel Dudley sends his compliments, sir," the sergeant said. "He wishes to speak with you, and I am to escort you to his office."

William eyed the soldiers' carbines. "Hoot. Did he think rifles were necessary?"

"I hope they are not, sir. He wants it clear this is an official request, not an idle invitation."

"I was on an errand for the marshal. Allow me to inform him of the reason for my delay." His torso twisted and he snorted a hog's curse.

One of the soldiers sniggered, and his partner shot him a warning look.

The sergeant stared into William's face for several seconds, his teeth worrying his lip. "It would be better if you just came along now. We'll let the marshal know if you're delayed for a spell."

"Am I under arrest?" William dropped his right hand slowly and arched his fingers over the butt of his gun.

The sergeant eyed the movement and sucked in a breath. "Would you be resisting if you were?"

"I would want to know the charge, and would turn myself over to the marshal."

The sergeant exhaled and pulled at his ear. "All right. Tell the marshal you'll be going with us to see the colonel. But make it quick."

William walked the few yards back to McAdams's

office and stepped inside. "Colonel Dudley sent soldiers to escort me to his office. Fiss, fiss. I wanted you to know in case I am not b-b-back by supper."

William closed the door and turned. Both carbines pointed at him.

"I hope this makes the urgency of the colonel's *request* clear and that there will be no more delays." The sergeant's lips formed a thin straight line.

"I understand the colonel. P-p-perfectly."

The soldiers relaxed their stances, and the rifles wavered, now only loosely aimed in his direction—a sign they couldn't make up their minds if he was a threat or not. "Take me to him."

"I think you know the way," the sergeant said. "We'll be right behind you."

William strode to the fort, and this time when he entered, the two sentries on duty took gawking notice of him. He gave them a little wave. He crossed the parade ground and stepped up to the door marked COMMANDER'S OFFICE. Before he could push it open, a restraining hand dropped on his shoulder.

"You have to give me your guns before you go in," the sergeant said.

"In that case, I will see the colonel out here." He stared the sergeant down. "I am never out of reach of my guns."

The sergeant raised a placating hand. "It's just protocol.

No armed civilians allowed. You'll get 'em back when you leave."

"Keep within arm's reach of me and I will let you c-c-carry them into the office." He grimaced and touched his shirt three times. "That is as unarmed as I get. If that is not good enough, we will have to conduct our business in the street."

Shrugging, the sergeant accepted William's guns, then pushed open the door and motioned William inside.

He stepped into the vestibule and waited while the sergeant rapped on an inner door.

"Come in," said a clipped voice.

"After you, sir." The sergeant motioned William through.

Two men waited in the room. Colonel Dudley sat at a ponderous wooden desk. White-haired and clean-shaven, he had a hawkish nose and beetling brows. Polished brass buttons and golden insignia flashed from his sharply creased uniform.

A thin man dressed in a black suit and string tie stood beside the desk. He smelled of talcum.

Stacked on the desk in front of the colonel gleamed five gold coins.

Rough Lodgings

Colonel Dudley smiled when he saw William staring at the coins. "You look surprised."

"You are the one p-p-paying for the hired guns to kill me?" He posed the question from the shock of the moment, for his mind told him it was not possible; gold coins first appeared in Trinidad, before he'd entered Lincoln County.

"Not me," Colonel Dudley said. "I'm just paid to make sure you don't leave town."

An oily smile slicked the lips of the man wearing the string tie. "Someone's on the way to meet you."

"Are you f-f-from the governor's office?" William asked the thin stranger.

"I'm Governor Axtell's aide, Leon Higgins."

William frowned in thought. "What does the g-g-governor want with me?"

"Nothing that he's told me about," Higgins said.

A snort escaped William. "Guess you are not that much of an aide to the governor, then."

Higgins shrugged and motioned for Colonel Dudley to continue.

The colonel picked up a folded paper from his desk and held it out for William to see. "This telegram came with the money. It says to hold you until an agent arrives to deal with you."

"What does that mean?" William shifted his attention from the colonel to Higgins. "Who is behind this?"

Higgins's pupils shifted to the corners of his eyes. "Governor Axtell didn't say."

Wariness, like hearing a rustle in the underbrush but not seeing the rattler, dried William's mouth. "So the governor is involved?"

Higgins shook his head. "Governor Axtell has no direct interest in you. He's being paid to see that you and a certain someone meet. Finding you here in Fort Sumner surprised me, so I telegraphed the governor for orders."

"That's enough talk for now," Colonel Dudley said. "William, you're confined to your quarters."

William laughed. "I am not a soldier. I have no quarters here."

"I'll have some assigned."

"I am a civilian; you have no authority over me."

"I am the commander of this post," Dudley said. "I have complete authority over all persons on the fort." He turned to Higgins. "Isn't that so?"

"Yep," Higgins drawled. "That's about the size of it."

"Sergeant." Colonel Dudley spoke to William's escort. "Lock up his revolvers in the armory for now."

"Hoot." William's knees buckled. He grabbed the desk to steady himself.

"Then come back here and take him to the BOQ," Colonel Dudley said, eyeing William askance.

The sergeant saluted and left.

William furrowed his eyebrows. "BOQ?"

"Bachelor officers' quarters," said Colonel Dudley. "Now sit down before you fall down."

"I have my own quarters," William said. "I am staying at the s-s-stable. Emmett expects me back soon."

"Sorry," Dudley said. "I don't want you to leave the fort until the agent, whoever he is, gets here."

"You mean I am a p-p-prisoner."

"A guest," Dudley said, returning the telegram to his desk. "By order of the governor. You may move around the post freely, but you will remain unarmed, and you can't leave."

William stared into Dudley's face. "Speak plainly, Colonel. The 'agent' is a g-g-gunfighter sent to kill me."

"What makes you so certain?"

William pointed at the stack of coins. "This is not the first such p-p-payment I have seen. When the man arrives, he will have f-f-five gold coins just like those."

Dudley considered this a moment. "We'll search him when he gets here. If he has the coins as you say, I'll return your revolvers. But until then, you remain unarmed."

Anger and fear chased each other through William's thoughts as he waited for the sergeant's return. He cursed himself for a fool. The marshal had warned him not to come onto the fort, though this time had not really been by choice. Still, he could have resisted his curiosity at what the colonel wanted and refused to let the sergeant take his guns—or insist the colonel either break his rule about armed civilians being allowed in his office or come outside to speak with him.

True, the soldiers had him at gunpoint, but he could have dealt with that. Maybe he would have been killed, but he would have gone down fighting. Now, unarmed, he stood in hostile territory, with a gunman coming to kill him. And what if one of the soldiers, or even Colonel Dudley himself, decided to collect the bounty on his head?

The sergeant returned and led him to a one-story adobe structure several doors away from Doctor Stone's office. Within the building, a hallway joined four rooms, two on each side. His escort ushered him into one. A plaque affixed to the door across the hall said CAPTAIN OATES. No sign hung on William's door.

The single-windowed room held a narrow cot, a wash-stand, a straight-backed wooden chair, and a pedestal table. The floor shone of freshly mopped wood and smelled of pine. Three empty shelves protruded from the whitewashed walls.

"Make yourself at home," the sergeant said. "Mess is at six in the morning and six at night." He pulled the door shut as he left.

William tried the latch. The door was not locked. He stuck his head out and saw the sergeant walking away down the hall.

The sergeant turned around, brows set in a firm line. "Yes, sir? Is there something else?"

"Would you go to the stable and t-t-tell Emmett why I will not be at work for the next few d-d-days?"

The sergeant turned and walked away, leaving William unsure if Emmett would be contacted.

That night William thought of going to supper for no other reason than to relieve the boredom of lying on his cot and staring at the ceiling. Without his guns, though, he decided to stay away from people.

Hunger had no room in his belly for the fear that roiled there. He was confined for at least one night, and if one of the troopers got wind of the bounty on his head, he was a sitting duck. He pushed the cot to the wall so that it was directly under the window and braced the chair under the doorknob.

He pulled the sheet from the cot and twisted it into a short rope, then knotted the end. A feeble weapon, but the best surprise he could arrange. When he sat in the corner, anyone attempting to shoot him through the window would have to stick the gun pretty far into the room. If so, William might disarm a man with a lucky snap of his makeshift sap.

His back wedged in the corner, knees drawn to his chest, William waited in the failing light. He focused his thoughts on the coming day, planning his moves should he live through the night.

Bet Your Life

William waited through the slowly passing hours until his bladder forced him to move. He pulled back the chair and eased open the door. The empty hallway looked safe.

He crept down the hall and gave a hasty look outside at the deserted parade ground. A glance at the stars told him the time was around three in the morning. He smelled biscuits baking. Taking a chance, he used the privy.

He returned to his room feeling more confident. Nevertheless, he rebraced the chair under the doorknob and returned to his vigilance from the corner. All right, he thought, the soldiers had showed no sign they were going to murder him.

The next threat was the gunfighter already on his way.

William risked breakfast the next morning, for if they hadn't tried to kill him during the night, the day was probably safe. A long table filled the center of the mess hall, and the soldiers filed past a serving line along one wall. There, three soldiers wearing aprons mottled with grease spots and flour slapped hot food onto tin plates. The scene reminded him of a chuck wagon on the open range, but all bound up and confined by adobe and stone.

He sat at the end of the one long table, as far from the other diners as he could. But soon his abnormal movements drew attention.

The corpulent corporal who had tried to draw on him during his last visit to the fort approached first. "What are you doin' here? This mess ain't for civilians."

An involuntary chuckle escaped William, and he stirred his oatmeal. "It is not fit for soldiers either."

The corporal glared at him.

William put down his spoon. "I am here by special invitation of Colonel Dudley. B-b-believe me, I would rather be someplace else."

"We heard about that," the corporal said. "But what're ya doin' in the mess hall? Eat your food in your room."

"You mean this place has room service?"

The corporal looked puzzled, but a soldier standing behind him laughed. Regaining his composure, the corporal said, "What I mean is I don't want to see you when I eat. All your jumping around and shit. It ruins my appetite."

William glanced at the corporal's fat middle and shrugged. "I will not be around much longer to trouble your digestion. There is a gunfighter coming, and the colonel is holding me for him."

"I can't wait to see that," the corporal said, relaxing his stance.

"What makes you think you will g-g-get to see it?" A shift in plans occurred to him. He had planned on using the soldiers' penchant for gambling to force Jesse to face him. But he had to take care of this gunfighter first. If played correctly, it might kill two birds with one stone. "Most likely I will be murdered in the night—no witnesses." William purposefully lurched, twisting his torso. "Too afraid to face me in a showdown."

"Who'd be afraid of you? You're just a clown with guns. I'd give a month's pay to see you stand up to a real gunfighter."

"Would you bet a month's pay against me?"

"In a flash."

William surveyed the circle of troopers that had gathered around them. "In a fair fight? A showdown?"

A chorus of agreement arose, the corporal's note the loudest. "But who'd bet on you?"

"I suppose it d-de-depends on the odds."

The corporal laughed. "I wouldn't bet on you at a hundred to one."

"Perhaps there are others less foolish," William said, all traces of humor gone from his voice. "At a hundred to one."

The troopers chatted excitedly among themselves at that and left William alone to finish his breakfast.

He bolted his food and left the mess hall to see Dudley. He waited in the front office until the colonel called him in, then strode to the colonel's desk.

"The soldiers are making b-be-bets on a showdown between me and the gunfighter who is coming."

Colonel Dudley frowned. "Who said there'll be a showdown?"

"History. A showdown is expected when two opposing g-g-gunfighters meet."

"How did they find out we're expecting a gunfighter?"

William shrugged. "Higgins, that man from the g-g-governor's office, seemed loose-lipped to me. All the soldiers at the mess this morning talked about the expected gunfight."

He bit the inside of his cheek to keep from smiling. He had told two truths from which the colonel drew a lie.

Colonel Dudley leaned forward over his desk and rubbed his right eyebrow with the palm of his hand. "I had hoped for a quieter resolution."

"You agreed to return my g-g-guns if this agent turned out to be a hired killer."

"Yes, I wouldn't give you unarmed to a man sent to kill you," Dudley said. "But I still hope the agent is just someone coming to take you back to see the governor."

William gave the colonel a wry smile. "Do you really believe that?"

The colonel sighed. "No, I don't."

"There is a way you can profit from this," William said.

Colonel Dudley folded his hands on his desk. "I'm listening."

"Make the showdown a public event. Encourage b-b-betting, and then you hold the stakes for t-t-ten percent. No matter who dies, you win."

Dudley stared ahead for a moment, his face a cipher. Then he met William's eyes. "How big a stake do you have—besides your life, I mean?"

"My horse and gear, my guns. Should fetch a c-co-couple of hundred."

"Are you telling me to sell them and stake the money?"

"No, I expect I will be n-n-needing them again. But if I do lose, then sell everything and split the proceeds amongst the winners."

"I couldn't count your things at full value if I'm just holding them. It's hard to take ten percent of a horse. But I'll credit you with a hundred into the kitty for them unsold."

William nodded.

"Not much of a stake on your side," Colonel Dudley said.

"Most of the soldiers will b-b-bet against me, so demand long odds. At ten to one, my stake will c-co-cover a thousand dollars bet against me."

"Doubt I can get any better than four to one. A trooper might bet a month's pay against a week's winnings, but accept no less a payoff than that."

William smiled, knowing he had roped the colonel. "Talk to Marshal McAdams. He will b-b-back me. Probably Emmett at the stable too."

"I'll see what I can scrape together." The colonel paused. "You know I'll bet against you."

Stakes

William laughed. "Go with the favorable odds and b-b-bet on me. More profit for you that way."

"A month of my pay would add considerably to the stakes on your side." Colonel Dudley pursed his lips, staring into the distance.

"One other thing," William said. "The gunfighter will have five gold pieces on him. Those are mine when this is over."

"Why?"

"Call it a side b-b-bet—even odds."

"And if you lose?"

"He keeps the g-g-gold. Think of the money as a prize for the winner of the contest between us." William stared hard into Dudley's eyes. "But I am not going to lose."

Colonel Dudley drew in a breath, held it, then relaxed, with a sigh escaping from his lips. "I like your confidence. I'll back you at four to one. Remember, though, when the other man is dead, I get ten percent of your winnings as well as my own."

"The one hundred you are s-s-staking me for my horse, guns, and gear at four to one, m-m-minus the forty-dollar holding fee. That means three hundred and s-s-sixty, plus the gunman's one hundred in gold, goes to me when he is dead." William held out his right hand to the colonel. "Agreed?"

Colonel Dudley grasped William's hand. "Agreed." Still holding William's hand in a firm grip, he added, "Provided the agent really does have the five gold coins. Otherwise, no gunfight, and he takes you back to the governor."

William smiled and withdrew his hand. "Start the wagering."

Colonel Dudley scowled. "How can you be so certain he'll have the gold? Even if he has been paid to kill you, he might've spent it already."

"In which case you will not b-b-believe me and turn me over to him, unarmed. He will k-k-kill me as soon as he gets me out of town." William measured Dudley's reaction. Good that the colonel looked worried about the possibility. "But the g-g-gold will be on him. If he has already spent it, then why r-r-risk his life and come at all? If whoever hired him pays in advance, then he t-t-trusts the killers he hires to complete the job."

"Assassins with honor," Colonel Dudley mused aloud. "I wonder where he gets such men."

William rubbed his chin with his left hand. "Have you spent the hundred you got with the telegram?"

The colonel smiled. "No. I figured I wouldn't earn it until I turned you over to the agent."

"There is some honor in all men." William held Dudley's gaze. "Even colonels."

Colonel Dudley knitted his brows, then gave a slight shrug. "I think I'll wager the hundred on you."

"And so profit from your honor." William turned to leave. Then, as if struck by an afterthought, he turned back. "Now that we are partners, how about you return my guns? It would cost you a lot of money if Jesse Evans k-k-killed me before the showdown."

Colonel Dudley's eyes narrowed. "But I don't want you running off either."

"I stand to make almost five h-h-hundred dollars by facing the gunman." William tottered for a moment, regained his balance. "And as long as Jesse Evans is still in the jail, I am not going anywhere."

"We'll compromise. You can leave the post, but I'll keep your guns locked in the armory."

"That would be dangerous for us if Jesse is r-r-released in the meantime."

"All right," Colonel Dudley said. "I'll see that Jesse Evans stays in jail until after the gunfight."

William relaxed with a sigh and nodded. "Fair enough. I will be working at the stable. You can find me there." He could always find another gun.

"I'll send the corporal."

"Better that you send the sergeant. The c-c-corporal does not seem to have the temperament for working with me."

Colonel Dudley scribbled a note on a blank form from a pad on his desk, tore it off, and handed it to William. "Show this to the guards at the gate."

William left the colonel's office and walked across the parade ground, heading for the gate. A sentry stepped forward to bar his way.

"Orders are that you ain't to leave the post." The soldier, whose beard stubble resembled brown grass poking up through melting snow, chewed on his lower lip.

"The colonel has changed those orders." William handed the colonel's note to the young man.

The soldier scanned the document and relaxed his pose. "You the one the wagerin's about?" He handed the paper back to William.

"Hoot." William smacked his own chin with the back of his hand.

"Ain't ya scairt?"

William grunted. "I do not have a gun, and there is a hired killer on his way. So yes, I am afraid."

"But you'll have a gun at the showdown."

"With a gun in my h-h-hand, I fear no man."

The sentry looked at him, the slant of his eyebrows registering doubt. "Have you ever gunfought before?"

"Yes." William tried to step around the sentry, who moved to block him once more.

"Do ya know who's comin'?"

William shook his head. "I do not know who they have sent."

"Then how do ya know you can beat him? He could be the fastest man alive."

"He is not," William said. "I am. You should bet on it. See the colonel." He stepped around the sentry once again and walked through the gate.

Stable Time

William stopped by the stable and glanced into the stall holding Jesse's horse. The sorrel looked back at him, then bent her neck to grab another mouthful of oats.

Emmett paused his straw pitching. "Where've you been?"

"The colonel restricted me to the f-f-fort last night, but I talked my way out this morning."

"Where're your guns?"

William twitched. "Locked up in the fort armory." William filled him in about the pending arrival of the gunslinger and the wagering on the outcome. "If I lose, they will come for my h-h-horse."

"Are you really gonna stay around and fight this man?"

"I am here for Jesse, and this fight is the p-p-price I am willing to pay to have my shot at him."

Emmett leaned on the shaft of his pitchfork. "The two don't necessarily go together."

"Yesterday, the c-c-colonel was against me, and Jesse could be released at any time. Today, the colonel is on my side, and has promised to keep Jesse around until after this business is settled. Agreeing to the showdown with the gunman accomplished all that."

"So you'll wait? What'll ya do in the meantime?"

"Keep working at the stable, if you still want me. Right after I have a t-t-talk with the marshal."

Emmett nodded. "Course you're welcome to stay."

"Thank you. I just need to fill in the m-m-marshal and I will be right back." He paused a moment. "Emmett, you have an extra g-g-gun around?"

A few minutes later, with the gun Emmett loaned him stuck under his belt, he strode to McAdams's office. When he pushed the door open, he found the marshal talking with Higgins, the governor's aide.

Higgins looked surprised. "I thought the colonel had you locked up."

William shook his head. "He changed his mind about r-re-restricting me to the post."

"That fool. He is supposed to make sure you don't leave town until the gunslinger gets here."

"Why is the governor taking such an interest in my comings and g-g-goings?"

Higgins bit his lip.

McAdams glowered at Higgins. "I don't like you and I don't trust Axtell. Sounds to me like he's part of a murder-for-hire deal. You better tell us what you know, or I'm gonna lock *you* up."

William pounded his fist on the desk. "Who is paying for this? Where is the g-g-gold coming from?"

Higgins paled. "Some lawyers from back east, and they're spreading it thick."

"Is the railroad behind this?"

Higgins looked perplexed. "What railroad?"

"The Denver and Rio Grande."

"I don't know." Higgins's eyes swung back and forth from William to McAdams. "All Governor Axtell told me is that it's money from eastern lawyers. Massachusetts, I think."

"You can relax. I am not leaving town so l-l-long as Jesse is here. If that means facing Axtell's gunman, so much the better. I want to find out whose gold is behind this." William tapped the middle button on his shirt three times. "Time we put a stop to it."

A Long-Awaited Duel

Two days later, as William and Emmett shoveled out the stalls in the early afternoon, a stranger rode up. The man sat easy in the saddle, relaxed as a mountain lion in the noon sun. A wide brimmed hat shaded his face, a short coat draped to his waist, and dark brown britches without chaps encased his legs. The sun-bleached grips of a Remington stuck out of a holster dangling from a worn belt draping the saddle horn.

Emmett went to meet him.

"Got room for my horse?" the man asked. "Probably just for one night."

Emmett shrugged. "Always got room for another horse. This is a corral, not a hotel."

The man slid his left boot from the stirrup, swung his

right leg over his saddle horn, and glided to the ground. At no time did his eyes stray from Emmett's face nor his right hand move far from his gun. "Meant no offense."

Emmett took a deep breath and released it. "Sorry. Town's been tense for the last few days."

"Oh? What about?"

"There's a showdown brewing, but we're one gunfighter short." Emmett looked closely at the stranger. "Or are we?"

The stranger smiled. "They say it's my eyes that give me away."

"Go talk to the colonel at the fort." Emmett scowled. "Your horse'll be waitin' for ya, if you'll be needin' it."

"Much obliged." The man swept his hat off to wipe his brow with his sleeve. "Torrey's the name. I'll be back."

"Think I heard o' ya. Don't folks call ya 'Two Shot'?"

The gunman smiled. "Tha's right. I get two shots off before mos' men get one." He left the stable.

When the man had gone, Emmett hurried to William.

"The gunfighter's here."

William nodded. "I saw him. I will go to the fort and g-g-get my guns."

"You know him?"

William laughed. "No, but I rarely meet a gunfighter more than once."

"This one's dangerous. Claims he's twice as fast as anyone else."

William snorted, then rubbed his jaw. "As Wyatt Earp has been known to remark, 'Fast is fine but accuracy is final.'" He waved a dismissive hand at Emmett. "I am not afraid of anyone who says he needs two shots."

Emmett's brows tented. "Let's go get the marshal; then we'll both go to the fort with you."

When they arrived at the marshal's office, they met McAdams coming from the side hall where the cells were located. "I know, Two-Shot Torrey's here. It's all over town." He scratched his chin. "Is it going to happen this afternoon?"

"Hoot. We cannot have the showdown until I get my g-g-guns."

McAdams pointed to Emmett's gun, which was still tucked under William's belt. "What about that one?"

"Almost forgot." William handed the gun back to Emmett. "Want my own rig for this. Thanks for the loan."

Emmett hesitated to take the gun. "Don't ya think ya should hold onto it a bit longer? Seems like you're walkin' into this unarmed."

William shook his head. "No need to c-c-cause things to get started prematurely. Until the showdown, it is safer if I am unarmed."

"I suppose there's no way to talk you out of this," McAdams said.

"What do you think?" He touched his shirt button

three times and started toward the door without waiting for an answer.

Emmett and McAdams flanked him, and the trio strode toward the fort.

They walked through the fort gates into an already excited crowd. New bets were shouted back and forth. William stumbled, and the odds went higher.

William winked at Emmett.

The three of them marched across the parade ground, knocked on the colonel's door, and pushed into the vestibule without waiting. Five soldiers milled about but parted to let William through to the inner office.

Colonel Dudley, standing behind his desk, was handing something to the stranger while Higgins smiled. The colonel looked up when William entered.

"Just as you predicted," the colonel said, "five twenty-dollar gold pieces. Sergeant, get William's guns from the armory, then call the men to formation."

"Hoot." His torso torqued. He and the gunman eyed each other.

"So you're the one all this fuss is about." The stranger smirked. "Looks like easy money to me."

The man, older and smaller than William, had taken off his coat. Trail dust soiled his shirt, which was frayed at the cuffs and collar. Six empty cartridge loops dotted the scuffed gun belt. His weathered holster, tied down to his thigh, hung from the belt. His double-action revolver nestled inside, its wooden grip worn smooth and poised perfectly at hand level. The man's hands were long fingered with prominent knuckles.

"You have to be the oldest g-g-gunfighter I have ever seen." William's shoulder jerked. "So you must be s-s-smart as well as fast. Why are you d-d-doing this?"

The man's eyes dulled. "Nothing personal. It's just a payday."

"You risk your life for a hundred dollars? That is making m-m-money the hard way."

"There's ten thousand dollars when you're dead."

"What? Who is paying that much? And why?" Anxiety opened a pit in his stomach. If true, the gunfighters would never stop coming.

The man stared, eyes locked onto William's. A race of bugle notes sounded, calling the soldiers to formation.

The fat corporal entered, carrying William's guns. "The sergeant told me to bring these," he said to the colonel. "Is it time?"

"Where's the sergeant?" Colonel Dudley asked. "I told *him* to fetch the guns."

"He told me to bring the guns, sir," the corporal said in clipped military cadence.

"Very well," the colonel said. "Gentlemen, follow me." He left the office.

The gunman followed.

William nodded and reached for his gun belts. The corporal handed him only the single-action Peacemaker. "The other man has only one gun. This is a straight-up fair fight."

"You might not have noticed his is a double action," William said.

The corporal smirked. "A gun's a gun."

The colonel called from outside. "William, what's keeping you?"

"Checking my gun, sir. It has been out of my possession for several days."

The corporal frowned. "I think you're just scared. Well, you can't get out of this now."

"Go on. Give my other gun to the colonel. Be out in five minutes."

After the corporal left, William stripped down his pistol and checked it. He found a small shim planted into the trigger spring that would slow its action. A slather of mud caked the inside of the barrel.

Not having his cleaning kit, he tore a strip from his shirttail and used a pencil from the colonel's desk to ram the cloth and clear the barrel. He reassembled his revolver, minus the extra shim. Then he replaced all of the bullets in the chambers with fresh ones from his belt.

It took a little longer than five minutes, making the

crowd outside restive. His appearance at the door drew a few catcalls.

A file of soldiers stood shoulder to shoulder, lining the street from the colonel's door toward the fort's entrance. The gunfighter stood at the end closest to the gate. Townsfolk pushed and shoved, a tumultuous tide held in check behind the dam of soldiers at parade rest.

The sergeant had positioned the line so the sun gave neither adversary an advantage.

William stepped off the boardwalk and stalked toward the gate. Shouted words of encouragement hushed as William approached to within fifty yards of the gunfighter. Had the stranger been in on the corporal's tampering with his gun? The thought, like a leaf before a storm, whirled around and around.

He strode forward.

The gunfighter stood still, waiting.

William took another step, calculating. This one's wily, he thought. Has me walking to him and will start his draw when my left foot is forward, with the weight on my right. That might cause my gun to stick a bit in the holster—and my hand be an inch out of position. Smart.

Forty yards between them. This gunfighter claimed he would make ten thousand dollars today. No doubt he'll try every trick. Like maybe befuddle me with lies of ten thousand dollars? Now I need him *alive*, to tell me what he knows. And all *he* needs to do is kill me. His stomach gave one flutter of butterfly wings.

Distracted, he almost missed it.

At thirty yards, as William still moved forward, the stranger's hand blurred in a lightning draw.

At the motion, his dark tornado descended.

A thunderclap.

His gun fired. The recoil punched up his arm.

Smoke obscured his view of the gunfighter.

A dust devil whirled up a yard to his left.

He wanted to fire again, but had no clear target.

His breath caught on a knife-edge as his finger froze in the very act of pulling the trigger.

He waited out the eternal seconds.

The blood stopped pounding behind his eyes, and his vision cleared. The stranger lay face up in the dirt. The certainty that his reputation had just gone up another notch—another nail in his own coffin—soured the sweetness of victory.

Amidst the hushed crowd, William walked to where the gunfighter lay.

The man looked up at him, his breathing labored. A ghost of a smile played about his lips. "I woulda sworn it was impossible to draw that fast and hit anythin'."

"You were fast, fast on the draw," William said.

Torrey groaned. "At thirty yards, I've always gotten a

second shot before the other fella got over the surprise." The man's breath whistled now, and his blood flecked his mouth. "Thissss time the ssssurprissse isssss mine."

The gunfighter's draw was as fast as William's own. Torrey was the first to ever actually get off a shot against him. The crowd shouted. William looked up; Doctor Stone hurried toward them. The doctor would be too late.

"Who sent you?" William asked the dying man.

The man's last breath leaked away. "Wa-shh-shhhhh …"

Doctor Stone knelt by the man, feeling for a pulse. Colonel Dudley and Marshal McAdams joined the tableau. Stone looked up and shook his head.

"Hoot damn hoot." William kicked at the dirt with the toe of his boot.

Dudley reached into the gunman's vest pocket and drew out the five gold coins. He handed them to William. "I've got to pay off the few that bet on you." The colonel winked a smile. "Come to the office later and I'll have your winnings."

"I would like my gun back now." He nodded toward the sergeant who had William's other gun belt slung over his shoulder.

"Sure. I did my part for the governor." He waved the sergeant over. Dudley headed for his office.

A tide of relief swept through him when he strapped on the second gun belt. Now for Jesse.

Jesse Repays a Debt

Was there really ten thousand dollars on his head? If so, more trouble surely headed his way. Perhaps the next hunter drew near even now. And no guarantee that the next one would come at him in an open fight. Lots of nooks and crannies around town were suitable for ambush. He had to finish with Jesse and move on.

Doctor Stone stood up, wiping his hands on the front of his pants.

"How is Jesse?" William asked.

Stone wrinkled his nose. "How's that? Oh, Mr. Evans." He turned to William. "He'll be a bit sore for a while, but I released him from my care." The doctor looked back at the dead man, then sighed. He called three soldiers over. "Let's get this man off the street. Take him to my office."

William turned to McAdams. "Are you ready to release Jesse?"

"Go collect your winnings, William." McAdams's voice was edgy and sharp. "You'll be wantin' some traveling money. Then come to my office."

"Sounds like you are ordering me out of town."

"We'll discuss it at my office."

"And *your* winnings?" William asked.

"I didn't bet. Wagering on a man's life—disgraceful, bad as the Romans with their gladiators. If I had jurisdiction on the fort, I'd lock up the lot of you."

"In that case, I b-b-better go with you to the jail now." William smiled. "I want to be there when you release Jesse."

McAdams clenched his jaw. "Too late. I released him as soon as I heard the gunfighter had arrived. If he took my advice, he's left town already."

William turned to Emmett. "Did he pick up his horse yet?"

Emmett shrugged. "I been with you the whole time since that gunfighter fella got here."

"Go back to the s-s-stable and check. If he has not left yet, s-s-stall him. I need one quick word with the colonel."

William rushed to the colonel's office and in his haste nearly collided with the young sentry with the brown stubbled beard as the man was exiting the building.

The young man smiled and waved some bills in William's face. "Took your advice. Thanks, mister."

William reached into his own pocket and pulled out a dollar. "Do me a favor. Buy that fat c-c-corporal a drink with my compliments. My way of saying thank you for taking such good care of my g-g-guns."

William passed through the vestibule and into Dudley's office. The colonel was smiling and whistling under his breath as he counted out money spread across his desk.

"You were right, William. Lot more profit in this your way." He handed William three hundred and sixty dollars in bills and coins. "And I get to keep the hundred dollars that came with the telegram."

William handed twenty dollars back to the colonel. "Let me know who claims the body of the man I just killed. See if they know who hired him."

Dudley gave William a long look. "Somebody is willing to pay ten thousand dollars for your head. Believe me, I'm interested in finding out who."

"So am I."

"Figured that name would be worth a lot to you. Say, twenty thousand."

William touched the side of his nose in mock salute. "I have as much chance of coming up with twenty thousand as you have of outdrawing me."

"I'll let you know if I learn anything," Dudley called after him. "Then you decide what it's worth to you."

William returned to the stable, glad to be out of the fort. The desert would grow peaches before he dealt with the military again. Except for that fat corporal. With him, he had unfinished business.

Emmett met William at the stable entrance. "The sorrel is gone. I found seven dollars and this tacked to the stall." He showed William a scrawled note:

For my horse's keep.—JE

"Jesse Evans." William spat. "Emmett, I will be l-l-leaving now. What do I owe you for *my* h-h-horse's keep?"

Emmett looked surprised. "Nothing. You agreed to work it off."

"I missed a day, thanks to the colonel."

"No matter. But I wish you'd stay on a spell."

"Thanks, but Jesse's trail is g-g-getting cold." He grabbed his tack and saddled Sunfish. "He has a two-hour head s-s-start."

"Which way do you figure he went?" Emmett asked.

William reached under Sunfish's belly to tighten the cinch strap. "Probably back to Lincoln. That is where his g-g-gang is, so far as I know."

Emmett scratched at the stubble under his chin. "You could ask around a bit—maybe somebody saw him leave."

"People were watching the g-g-gunfight. I will take my chances that he is headed to Lincoln. If I hurry, maybe I can c-c-catch him before he gets there."

Emmett shook his head. "That sorrel mare of his looked to be as much horse as yours. If you ride fast enough to catch him, your mount'll be spent by the time you do."

"That situation is not improving as I s-s-stand here," William said. "Thanks for everything, Emmett."

"You might keep an eye out for that government fella," Emmett said. "He lit out of here headin' north after the gunfight. Practically ran me down in that fancy buggy of his."

"Have to wait until l-l-later." He swung into the saddle. "I am going south." He trotted Sunfish out of town.

William rode for hours. At times, he leaned forward in the saddle, one eye on the trail, searching for clear hoofprints in the exposed dirt. Then he sat back, gave looser rein to Sunfish, and urged his mount forward at a gallop until another patch of road showed clear prints.

An early spring thaw dappled the open meadows with Indian paintbrushes. The trail meandered among rounded hills now frosted with green. A lark, hidden in the low scrub beside the road, called to its mate.

William had just pulled Sunfish to a walk when a chip blasted off a boulder at the trail's edge. The shard struck Sunfish, causing the horse to rear. Only then did William hear the report of a rifle.

William tumbled off the back of his horse and rolled into scrub cover, startling the lark.

Sunfish darted farther down the road.

William waited, counted his breaths. At fifty, he began to crawl forward.

A bullet whined overhead, followed by another crack of the rifle. A scan of the surrounding hills disclosed no telltale puff of smoke. He left his guns holstered, the shooter way out of range for his revolvers. He needed the rifle still in its sling on his horse's back.

A third bullet kicked up a geyser of earth three feet ahead of him. He sprang up and sprinted for the cover of a stunted tree on the opposite side of the road. A fourth rifle shot, but this one must have gone wide as it left no mark of its passing.

Crouching behind the sparse limbs, he congratulated himself on getting a few feet closer to Sunfish. His mount grazed on the tough grass ahead, still out of reach.

"William!"

The call of his name carried on the wind, the sound tattered. Jesse's voice?

"William, can you hear me?" The same voice, coming

from the brushy hill ahead on his right. In the same direction as Sunfish.

"I hear you," William shouted. "What do you want?"

"Stand up, put your hands away from your sides, and step out where I can see you."

"I like it where I am." William scanned the hill, looking for the speaker, still wondering if it was Jesse.

"I just want to talk," the voice said. "If I'd wanted to kill you, I would've."

"If it is a p-p-parlay you want, you show yourself first." William squinted toward the source of the voice. "You have the advantage."

"I see your rifle still slung on your saddle," the voice said. "How far can you shoot with those handguns of yours, I wonder?"

The voice paused long enough for the crickets to begin.

"Stand up, or I'll shoot your horse."

Shoot Sunfish? William jumped to his feet without another thought. He stood, hands raised, every muscle tensed.

"That's better." Jesse stepped from behind a scrub oak. "I'm coming closer so I don't have to shout. Just keep your hands where I can see 'em."

William slowly folded his arms across his chest. He forced himself to take deep breaths as Jesse moved nearer.

No longer pointing the rifle directly at William, the outlaw picked his way down the hillside. Jesse stopped a hundred feet away and gestured with the rifle, pointing it loosely in William's direction. "I want you to stop following me," he said.

"I will." William dropped his arms to his side. "Once you are dead." The internal tornado built, unbidden but exhilarating.

"I don't know why you didn't just shoot me when I was locked up." Jesse sighted down the rifle at William. "Whether it was the marshal that stopped you, or your own honor . . . But I want to repay you."

The tornado screamed closer.

Jesse swung the rifle away from William. "I can tell you about the coins."

"Hoot." This he had to hear. William hugged his arms tight to his chest and throttled back his internal tornado a fleasnap before it exploded. His legs buckled involuntarily, pitching him to the ground.

He lay defenseless.

Jesse laughed.

Priorities

illiam closed his eyes, wondering if he would hear the shot that killed him. If this was where it ended, then at least once, he—and not the tornado—had made the choice.

Nothing happened. His racing pulse slowed. He opened his eyes and looked up at Jesse standing only ten feet away.

Shaking his head, Jesse peered at him, the rifle pointed toward the ground to William's right. "You're a strange one, William. If'n ya hadn't had your arms crossed, I'd have figured ya were making a play for your gun. But you're damn lucky I didn't shoot ya anyway."

William got to his feet. Wariness crossed Jesse's face; William kept his hands away from his guns. He smiled tightly. "Any more favors you owe me?"

Jesse laughed. "Nope, just this one. Ya spared my life in that cell back there. I'm sparing yours on the road today. I always pay my debts. Now we're even."

William dropped his hands to his sides. "We are not even. I still owe you for Tunstall."

Jesse stopped smiling. "I know he was your friend, but you've killed some of my friends, so that debt's already squared."

Was that the way of it? Had there been enough killing? Nothing would bring Tunstall back, or his sweetheart Emily either. At the thought of her, like the sudden clashing of warm and cold fronts, the tornado stirred in him again.

"I do not think the debt is p-p-paid." William teetered for a moment. "Let us finish it today."

"Not today." Jesse shifted the rifle slightly. "If I can't talk ya out of a gunfight, then let's at least wait until there's some money in it."

"I have five hundred d-d-dollars in my pocket. Make your play."

Moving carefully, Jesse bent at the waist and laid his rifle on the ground. He raised his hands in the air as he stepped over the weapon. "I won't kill you unless I have witnesses."

The tornado vanished from William's mind. Amazed, he stared at Jesse. "Why would you care about witnesses?"

"So no one disputes my claim." Even with his hands in the air, Jesse remained relaxed, confident.

"What claim? Are you l-l-looking to build a reputation?"

"There's ten thousand dollars on your head." Jesse turned his back on William and bent to retrieve his rifle. "Payable for killing ya in a gunfight. In front of witnesses."

"Payable by whom?" William inched toward Sunfish.

"Some lawyer back East." Jesse slung the barrel of his rifle over his shoulder.

"That much I know," William ground out. "What is the lawyer's name?"

Jesse tilted his head to one side for a moment. "He sends a telegram and five twenty-dollar gold pieces. The telegram has his name and how to contact him to collect the fee."

"So what is his name?"

"I haven't gotten the telegram myself—yet. Figure it's cuz I've been locked up. But now that I'm out, I expect to hear from him soon. So ya see, I don't want to shoot ya today, not when there's a lot of money in it later."

"What is the b-b-business of the five coins all about if the price on my head is ten thousand?" William reached Sunfish and stroked the horse's neck, eyeing the slung rifle.

"Just calling cards, I guess." Jesse put two fingers in his mouth and whistled. "So ya know you're facing a hired gun. Supposed to worry ya or something."

"If you have not gotten a t-t-telegram yourself"—he grasped the saddled horn for support—"how do you know so m-m-much about it?"

"Higgins told me." Jesse shaded his eyes with his hand to watch his horse trot toward him. He snatched the reins when the sorrel drew close. "That aide to the governor wanted a finder's fee to pass the name along, so he kept some details to himself."

"Did you pay him his fee?"

"Hell no." Jesse laughed. He pushed his rifle into its sling. "I don't need Higgins's help. I expect there'll be a telegram waitin' for me in Lincoln. I stopped ya on the road to pay my debt. Now we'll be even when next we meet. I'll gun ya down in front of witnesses. A clown like you is hardly worth the bother, but the ten thousand makes it so."

"Who is b-b-behind this?" William asked, anger and frustration trembling his voice.

"That answer lies in Trinidad." Jesse swung into his saddle. "Go find out if ya must and then we'll meet. I'll be waiting in Lincoln." Without a backward look, Jesse rode down the trail.

Instead of vaulting into the saddle himself, William stroked Sunfish and reviewed his options until long after Jesse left. He was reluctant to return to Trinidad and not just because of the distance and time lost. Remembering the coach ride with Emily over Raton Pass opened up old wounds.

If he went to Lincoln to settle with Jesse, he'd get swallowed up in that war again. It could be months before a chance came to return to Trinidad, and the trail to whoever put a price on his head started there. The killers would keep coming until the bounty was lifted, or he was dead. But every time he killed one of them his reputation got bigger and trapped him deeper in his life as a gunfighter.

How did it come to this? His illness kept him from getting close to people, but he had never wanted to be a killer. Becoming one had been forced on him. He remembered his first killing, back in Wichita. At that time, he had just played the hand he'd been dealt; now, after three years, he enjoyed pulling the hidden ace of his fast draw whenever required.

In truth, that life ate at his soul, day by day turning him into a killer. It was time to stop feeling anger at his condition and just blasting his way out of whatever situation confronted him. Jesse put it best days ago; his illness was a stagecoach and he was just along for the ride. Could he take the reins, or better yet, get off the coach? He'd always have his illness, but could choose not to let it make him bitter. Until then, he was like a whirlwind chewing up the horizon, deadly and alone.

He smiled at the irony of it. Jesse had put the first gun in his hand. Jesse was the man against whom he sought vengeance for the deaths in Lincoln. Now Jesse's stage-coach comment broke the marked trail for reclaiming William's soul. To top it all, settling with Jesse one way or another had to wait. For now.

His mind made up, he climbed into the saddle and without hesitation set Sunfish on a northern course. Somewhere in the rolling terrain ahead lay the road that connected Santa Fe with Fort Sumner. If he could find it. Once he struck that road, he'd take it to Santa Fe. If the railroad had reached there, he would stable Sunfish and take the train to Trinidad. And hope the governor didn't find him first.

If the tracks had not been laid as far as Santa Fe, he would ride toward Trinidad until he came to wherever the track had gotten. He and Sunfish could ride the rest of the way from there—the small cost worth saving Sunfish the rigorous trail down the pass.

The first part of his journey lay through the monoto-nous New Mexico high desert. He rode through an unforgiving landscape. Stunted trees splattered the undulating hills like buckshot. Every hill looked like every other. The chill wind sapped his senses one by one. The air, sucked dry by the cold, numbed his nose and turned his throat into a rasp. The reins became a dead weight on his fingers. The soft fall of Sunfish's shod hooves sounded in the spans between the wind's moans.

He steered by the westering sun. If he missed the road in the dark, he could wander as far north as Colorado before he got set right. And this day did not have much daylight left.

When the sun's rayed fingers caressed the horizon and turned the long landscape of small scrub into a forest of shadows, William saw a dirt road ahead. Nothing more than parallel tracks of hardened earth scoured into the rocky soil, but relief and pride on navigating over the unmarked wilderness coursed through him.

He hauled dried branches and built a pile by the side of the road. With a fire going, he made camp for the night.

The road ran east to west, and the next morning he rode with the sun behind him. Santa Fe, home to the governor, lay ahead. He doubted the governor expected him there, but if he was recognized, Axtell would put men on him pretty fast. And he was not hard to recognize.

He wished he could talk to the governor about the telegram from back East. Talk, though, could turn to gunplay. He'd become an officially wanted man. Posters with his name and picture all over the West. And the price on his head? What did they pay for a man who killed a governor?

Better to find out what Trinidad held for him. And hope.

The High Cost of Beer

The trail meandered through dome-shaped brown hills that grew higher to the north. The road turned in that direction and climbed upward at a steady grade. Scrub oaks gave way to dwarf pine. William rested Sunfish in a patch of verdant grass by a pool of water. Bird song punctuated long periods of silence. The air, crisp as a mountain spring, felt virgin.

But William did not relax. Though he did not intend to linger in Santa Fe, he would need to go to the train station there. And stable Sunfish until the business in Trinidad, Colorado, finished. Could he slip in and out of the city before coming to the governor's attention?

Sunfish refreshed, William continued his journey until entering the town of Lamy. Though small, it reminded him of Trinidad. Freight wagons outnumbered the buildings, and stacks of ties and iron rails pyramided everywhere.

He arrived in late afternoon. At the freight station ahead, barrels lined up along one wall. A heavily muscled man groomed a team of horses.

William rode up to him. "How far is it to Santa Fe?" he asked, concentrating hard to keep his tics at bay.

"'Bout fifteen miles," the man replied in a raspy voice without missing a stroke of his brush.

"Can I catch the train there?"

The curry brush stopped midsweep. "You must be a stranger to these parts. Railroad's not going to Santa Fe; it'll be coming through Lamy instead."

"Hoot. You are talking about the Atchison, Topeka and *Santa Fe?*"

"None other," the man said. He gave William a cursory look-over, and then returned to his currying. "Track should reach here this summer, then push on to Albuquerque."

"What about Santa Fe?" William wondered if somehow the governor was behind the change in route, but he couldn't discern the motive. Whatever it might be, it relieved William of the need to go to Santa Fe.

"Maybe Santa Fe'll get a spur line someday. The terrain's pretty rugged up there, and bypassing it now is an easier—and quicker—build." Finished with the brushing, the denim-clad hostler measured out oats from one of the barrels.

"How f-f-far to the head-of-track from here?" William grimaced at the tic that slipped through his guard and saw the man's eyes widen as he took note.

"Track's just this side of Raton Pass. Where're you lookin' to go?"

The man's sudden interest gave William pause. Had his tic given him away? Who all knew about the ten thousand gold pieces? "To the train." William tipped his hat. "Thanks."

"It's gettin' late. You can't get nowhere better'n Lamy by sundown." The man's unshaven face smiled up at William. "There's a boardin' house for us muleskinners down the street. I'm sure they'd have room."

"Got to feed my horse first."

"You'll find a stable next to the boardin' house."

William pointed at the barrel of oats. "I'll buy some of that feed from you."

"Help yourself," the man said. "Then lets you 'n me have a drink."

William dismounted and filled a saddlebag with oats for the journey to Trinidad. He paid with a silver dollar and remounted. "I have to push on, but I will buy you a drink for your help." He fished another dollar coin from his pocket and handed it to the muleskinner. "Thanks again."

"But . . ." the man started in his raspy voice.

William rode away. The muleskinner was probably harmless, and there was nothing wrong with staying the night in Lamy. But why take chances?

The right-of-way for the coming tracks had been carefully laid out and graded. The route led north and bypassed Santa Fe. Using this roadbed as his guide, he rode four hours before making camp.

Another night spent alone in a chill wind.

Up with the sun, William followed the marked route through increasingly rugged territory. The trip from Trinidad to Lincoln by stagecoach had taken a different route than this freshly carved one. Railroads always picked their way along the easiest path, but still, Sunfish grew tired and had eaten the last of the oats that morning.

William pushed doggedly onward through the rest of the day, passing up places to camp even though the hour grew late. He needed to find a town and knew that sooner or later the railroad route had to pass through one. He prayed for it to be soon.

Piano plinking and the murmur of conversation, punctuated by raucous laughter, gave notice of answered prayers. A building materialized from the gloom, and flickering lamplight spilled through a set of batwing doors. At least he'd found a saloon.

However, a gathering of inebriated men was not his top priority. A stable, sharing some food with the hostler, sounded much better. He thought of Emmett and sighed. He passed a sign that was difficult to read in the twilight: SPRINGER. If a town was big enough to have a name, it was big enough to have a stable.

When he found it, the locked doors and darkened interior meant the stableman wasn't there. Probably back at the saloon. There was a corral in back of the stable, and William led Sunfish to it. He pondered taking his tack off to let Sunfish rest, but caution told him to keep his mount saddled.

A trough held water, and hay filled the rick, so Sunfish was fine for the moment. No choice now but to find the owner of the stable. He walked back to the saloon.

The noisy piano music continued without falter when he pushed through the saloon doors. He leaned with his back to the bar near the doorway and surveyed the occupants. A few saloon girls circulated among knots of grizzled men.

"What'll ya have?" the bartender asked.

"Beer," William said, turning to look at the bartender. "Been a long ride."

The bartender nodded and drew liquid foam into a glass. "Want another? Might as well draw it while I'm standin' here."

William placed a dollar on the bar. "However much this will get me."

The bartender let the money lie. "Haven't been around here before, have ya? You're already two bits behind."

William dug out a quarter. "This the only saloon in town?"

"'Tis," the bartender said. "Expect more'll come with the railroad. Somethin' 'bout it ya don't like?"

Yes, he thought, but said, "Just looking for someone. Wondered if there might be another s-s-saloon to check."

At William's tic, the barman gave him a sideways look. "Who ya lookin' for?"

"The man who runs the stable. I want to feed my h-h-horse."

The barman relaxed. He pointed to a stocky man wearing suspendered pants and drinking with a hostess. "That's Big Jim. Looks like he's a might busy now."

"Is there somewhere in town I can get some f-f-food?"

"Got some beans in a pot in the back. I'll grab ya a bowl while ya wait."

"How much?" William asked.

"Five dollars."

"No thanks." Guess he'd go hungry tonight. "I'll just settle my business with Big Jim and go find s-s-someplace to sleep."

"I wouldn't bother him just now, but suit yerself." The

bartender moved down the bar to another patron who had started banging his mug on the wooden top.

Big Jim looked up, frowning when William approached. "What do *you* want?"

William smiled; he tried to make his eyes cooperate. He wasn't sure they did. "I need to stable my horse for the night. No need to brush him down—I will take care of that. I have already put him in the corral."

"Then what're ya bothering me fer?" Big Jim said, voice gruff. He slid his hand down the backside of the hostess. "I'm busy."

The hostess smiled at Big Jim and whispered in his ear.

"Okay. I will pay you in the m-m-morning, then." William grimaced and grabbed the table.

Big Jim's eyes, which had been looking at the waitress, turned to William. "What are ya, some kinda idiot?" he asked with a hostile glare. "Maybe ya best pay me now."

"All right." William reached for his pocket with his left hand. "How much?"

Big Jim looked at the half-empty bottle of whiskey on his table and then at the brunette hostess. He winked at her. "Ten dollars."

"Hoot." His hands trembled, and he fought to stave off the involuntary motion. No matter what he did, it felt as if his dark tornado was pushing him.

"Don't just stand there, fool," Big Jim said, puffing out his chest and smirking to the hostess. "Pay up or leave."

William's smile settled now like the cold curve of a steel plow. "Ten dollars. For my horse, rations of oats for t-t-tonight and tomorrow, and I will sleep in your h-h-hayloft." He extended a ten-dollar bill to Big Jim. "I will be gone in the m-m-morning."

Big Jim's smirk seemed to die a little, but he snatched the ten from William. "Now leave me alone."

William continued to hold out his hand, now emptied of the ten-dollar bill, palm up. "The key to the stable? Or w-w-will you escort me?"

Big Jim glared and the hostess stood up as if to leave. "Wait, Doreen," he said to her. To William he said, "Wait at the bar. I'm not through here yet."

William shook his head. "I am tired. I p-p-paid you, in advance. I will l-l-let myself in."

Hooking his arm tighter around Doreen's waist, Big Jim said, "Do what ya want. So long as you leave me and Doreen in peace."

William slogged back and led Sunfish out of the corral and around to the front of the stable. Eyeing the padlock that hung there, he gave it an experimental tug. He shrugged and shot off the lock.

Turning back to study the saloon, he waited. His shot brought no curious stares from over the batwing doors.

No one, not even Big Jim, gave it a scout. William walked Sunfish into the stable and found an open stall.

After giving his horse a quick rubdown and oats from a bin, William unfurled his bedroll in the mow and fell asleep before his third breath.

He dreamed of black tornadic clouds piling up and obscuring the horizon. Voices: Big Jim, Jesse, Two-Shot Torrey taunted from the dark depths. "You'll never be free of us." Then a dream sun rose *in the north* like a gold coin and burned away the clouds.

Trail to Trinidad

The next day William reached the railhead. The camp poised hungry-eyed, seeking to devour the miles before it, the trail behind as forgotten as scat.

Track had been laid through the pass, and a small depot rooted, mushroom-like, where the grade leveled out. No buildings had been erected, though lean-tos protected some of the material that lay in ordered rows. A circus-sized tent served as a saloon, diner, and flophouse.

Men toiled on half-empty flatcars, transferring rails and wood and kegs of spikes to wagons while teams of hobbled horses grazed on the high meadow grass. A steam engine chuffed and belched a black snake of smoke. William gritted his teeth at the ghostly reminder of past entanglements.

His tongue prickled in anticipation of someone calling his name, pulling him back to old ties to the railroad. His mouth dried to creosote, and his pulse pounded like sledges on spikes until the camp was behind him. The right-of-way followed the old stage road and led north from camp, back down through the pass to Trinidad. Grateful to be ignored, William rode on.

The roadbed held to a constant grade, and he used it where he could. In some places the rutted stage road ran alongside and at others the rails lay atop it. The fresh ties provided good footing for Sunfish, and he made good time.

He rounded the sweeping curve marking the exit from the pass and saw Trinidad spread below him. Though he'd only been gone a month, the face of the city had changed. Well-dressed people walked the streets, three or four new buildings had sprouted, and some of the old ones sported new brass fixtures and fancier signs. Trinidad purred less frenetically, more prosperously, like a contented cat.

William rode in and hitched Sunfish to the rail in front of the Topeka Lil. The saloon still smelled of sawdust and stale beer. Three men occupied one table; upward-turned chairs covered the others. The bartender, Sugar, glanced up when William entered the saloon.

Sugar returned to wiping down the bar, and then he looked up suddenly at William. "My lord, look who's back. Hot rum?"

"No thank you. Too warm a day for it." William motioned to the room. "Business fallen off?"

Sugar shrugged. "Still get the railroad men in here when they're in town. Local trade's coming back."

"The town has changed." William's fingers drummed the bar top. "New b-b-brass fittings on the buildings and new paint everywhere."

Sugar nodded. "Lots of fancy folk moving in. Ya know there's a doctor here now? Funny kind of doctor—calls hisself a specialist; opened an office on Main Street. Only treats diseases of the gut. Now what kinda doctor's that?"

William nodded and looked around the barroom again. "So, Sugar, do you remember that b-b-business with the hired gun a month ago? The one paid five twenty-dollar gold pieces?"

"Sure do. For a while there I thought it was your pal Dave Rodabaugh hired on to kill you."

"Dave and I worked together, but we were never p-p-pals." William leaned across the bar. "I am more interested in who did the hiring."

"Everyone knows it was the Denver and Rio Grande Railroad put up the money." Sugar blinked rapidly and rubbed his chin. "Wasn't it?"

"They offered five gold pieces. Now the bounty is ten thousand dollars. Is the railroad putting up that kind of money?"

Sugar whistled through his teeth. "Ten thousand? I ain't heard nothing 'bout that."

"Any D and RG men still in town? A representative I can t-t-talk to?"

"Nope, they pulled up stakes. Could still be some of their old tracklayers around, looking for work. Ya might find 'em at the Rio." Sugar pointed across the street. "You remember the Rio?"

"I remember it. Nearly burned down as I recall. Surprised to see it is still here."

"They rebuilt it fancier than ever. Put in roulette wheels and other games of chance." Sugar sighed. "No cloud but that don't have a silver lining."

The perpetually dark cloud of William's affliction might have had a silver lining once, but it had begun to tarnish. His speed with a gun kept him alive but didn't improve his life. The ten-thousand-dollar bounty over his head meant men would keep coming for him, until he was dead.

"Games of chance? I may have to go p-p-play a hand." William drew his Peacemaker and rolled the cylinder, checking each chamber. He smiled at Sugar. "Got a full deck."

Sugar nodded. "I'm sure the old Denver crew remembers not to draw to your hand. Good luck."

William marched across the street and pushed through the Rio's doors. The place had definitely seen improvements.

Felt-lined gaming tables now dominated one side of the room. A new brass rail gleamed at the bar, and behind it, a mirror with etched scrollwork decorated the wall. A score of gamblers were already hard at work.

William moved to the bar. Keeping an eye on the room in the mirror, he called the bartender over.

The barman chewed the corner of his lip as he looked William up and down. "What's your pleasure?"

William grimaced, lurched, and stuttered. He took a deep breath and patted the bar with his palm. "I would like a beer, and while I am drinking, a few w-w-words with you."

Watching William's odd movement, the barman frowned. "Are you sick or just real thirsty?"

"Either way, a beer will help." William smiled, feeling relief. The man neither remembered nor recognized him. He took the foaming glass put in front of him and laid a dollar on the polished-oak bar top.

The barman looked down at the coin. "How many beers?"

"Just this one."

"I'll get your change." He swept up the coin.

"Keep it," William said. "Are there any men from the D-D-Denver and Rio Grande here?"

The barman's eyes narrowed. "Um, you mean the railroad? They left town a month ago."

"I know the men from that line used to drink here. I need to speak to someone from the railroad. I hoped the Rio Saloon still had connections."

The bartender shook his head. "None that I know of, but then I've only been here a couple o' weeks."

William turned his back to the bar. The gamblers remained engrossed in their games. No one paid him any attention. The Rio Saloon had moved on. He left his half-finished beer on the bar and walked out the batwing doors.

Disappointed that he couldn't contact anyone from the railroad directly, William drew up a mental list of those who might know something: Sheriff Woolton, who kept his fingers on the pulse of what went on in Trinidad; stage-line owner Mr. Barlow, whose employee Copper had been the first to take the five gold pieces; and the Hotel Sherman barman, Samuel, who knew much of the business dealings of the town.

Of the three, Barlow was the man most directly linked to the first attempt on his life, and William decided to talk to him first. While legging it to the stage office, William recalled the last meeting he'd had with the man. Barlow had showed little remorse that his man Copper had mistakenly killed the reporter Washburn. He had been more concerned that William leave town as soon as possible. At the time, William thought Barlow's actions came from contrition over his unwitting role in the shooting. But could it have been that Barlow was behind the shooting and didn't want William poking around too much?

The stage office looked the same, though the hard chairs had been replaced with cushioned ones. A young Mexican who stood in Copper's old spot behind the counter turned a warm smile on William.

William smiled back. "I would like to speak to Mr. Barlow."

"I am very sorry, *señor*, but Mr. Barlow is not here today. Is there anything with which I could assist you?" The young man enunciated every syllable with care and little accent.

"My business with Mr. Barlow is p-p-personal." William's head jerked and he grabbed the counter for support. "When will he return?"

The clerk's mouth pouted sadly for a brief moment as he watched William's odd movement. "He spends much of his time in Denver," he said after William regained control. "I am afraid I do not know when he will return."

William sighed. He remembered taking a more aggressive stance when Copper gave him much the same answer. Had the clerk thought him rude at the time? Had the unintentional slight prompted Copper to be the first to try for the bounty on William's head? He didn't want to make that mistake again.

"I am sorry to hear that," he told the clerk. "Perhaps I can reach him by t-t-telegraph. To which hotel should I send the wire?"

"Mr. Barlow has a home in Denver, but I am sure you can reach him at our Denver office."

Perhaps the trail leads to Denver, William thought. He thanked the clerk and left.

He slogged over to Woolton's office. A dog-eared paper stuck on a nail in the door read, *Making rounds. Have a seat or leave a note.* Unsure of how long he'd need to wait for the sheriff, William returned to the Topeka Lil and unhitched Sunfish.

"Let me get you settled at the livery." He stroked his horse's neck. "Maybe for a few days." If he had to go to Denver, he would go by train.

After stabling Sunfish and filling the feed bag with grain, William returned to Woolton's office. This time he found the round-bellied scion of law and order sweeping out the cells.

Woolton frowned. "What're you doing back in town?"

William tapped his own shirt buttons three times. "Looking for answers."

"To what questions?" Woolton set the broom in a corner and moved to his desk.

"Someone has put a bounty of t-t-ten thousand dollars on my head. I want to know who and why."

"And you came back to Trinidad for that? There're no answers here."

Reunions

"The trail starts here. The f-f-first bounty hunter, Copper, was here. The s-se-second, a man I killed in Lincoln, said he had s-s-started looking for me here." William saw Woolton's eyes twitch like they were running for cover behind his eyelids. "A third got his orders through the governor's office in Santa Fe. They tracked me from here and into New Mexico."

Woolton let out a deep sigh. "I hoped we were quit of you."

"You will be as soon as I get my answers. No reason to stay." William bent and tapped Woolton's desk three times. "The man I killed in Lincoln, the one who said he came through Trinidad, wore a lot of black and silver. A skinny man with a face like a b-b-blade. What do you know of him?"

"I remember him asking around about how Washburn got kilt. Looked like trouble. I was glad he left. Not surprised he's dead, nor sorry, neither."

William straightened. "Washburn, the reporter?"

"Yes, the one who got kilt the night you shot it out with Copper." Woolton fixed his stare on William. "And I hope nobody else dies just because you're back in town."

"What happened after I left? Did you notify Washburn's family?"

"Of course. Telegram's here somewhere." Woolton sidled to a wooden filing cabinet and opened a drawer. His fingers pianoed through the files until he snatched out a pale yellow sheet of paper, which he handed to William.

On the form for outgoing telegraph messages, William read:

> *Regret to inform you that Kendrick Washburn killed in gunfight last night. Please wire instructions for body.*
> *Woolton, Sheriff*
> *Trinidad, Colorado*

"They contact you?" William pondered the message. "You ever tell them the whole story?"

"They just had me ship the body back to Massachusetts." Woolton thought a moment. "What do you mean 'the whole story'?"

"Your telegram makes it sound like he was part of the gunfight, not shot in the back by mistake."

Woolton took the message from William's hand. "You pay for telegrams by the word, so I'm not making a full tale of it." He read it again. "Hummph. I guess that is a bit confusing."

"Kendrick was a nice fellow. Write his family a letter and give them the details: he was not carrying a gun and he was shot in a case of m-m-mistaken identity."

Woolton shrugged. "Seems a bit late to go stirring things up after his family's put him to rest and all. Best let things be."

"They deserve to know the truth." William tossed a thoughtful look out the window. "Why was that gunman asking about Washburn's death? I think somebody was already stirring things up."

After Woolton agreed to write the letter, William sauntered to the hotel. The window through which Washburn had been shot sported new glass with white roses etched in the corners and SHERMAN DINER in gold lettering.

Robert stood on duty behind the front desk and stared, eyes dark craters in a pale moon face, when he saw William. The clerk waved one tremulous hand as William passed.

William nodded and turned for the dining parlor. He

spied Samuel in a starched white uniform; he was putting away glassware beneath a mirror-backed bar.

As William approached, Samuel placed an amber-filled glass on the solid oak counter. "Bourbon, sir?"

"Thank you, Samuel." William picked up the glass. "How have you been?" His hand shook as he picked up the bourbon and spilled a drop on the bar.

Samuel didn't blink, but whisked away the spill with a smooth motion of the hand towel. "I've been fine, sir. How is Miss Tunstall?"

William grimaced. "She has gone back to England."

"I'm sorry to hear that. The West is not for everyone."

"I think she realized that the night Washburn d-d-died."

"That was a horrible affair." Samuel picked up a decanter. "More bourbon, sir?"

William shook his head. He looked across the room to the table where Emily and Washburn sat that night. A new table, of heavier wood and more darkly stained, occupied the space now.

Samuel followed William's gaze. "They've improved the décor. Town's growing—no one wants to dwell on the past."

"Anyone shown any interest in these killings?"

"There was one man. Uncouth fellow, dressed in black and silver, fingering his guns when he talked, like they made his questions more important."

The back of William's neck prickled. "What did he want?"

Samuel leaned into the bar. "He kept asking all sorts of things about the shooting. When he found out you were the only survivor, he asked about you: who you were, what you looked like, where you went."

"What was his connection with the Denver and Rio Grande Railroad?"

"None I could tell. He worked for somebody else."

William placed his empty glass on the bar, confusion plowing furrows in his forehead. "I know Copper was given five gold p-p-pieces to kill me, and *that* money came from the D and RG. Then a fellow tracks me down to Lincoln and *he* has five gold pieces. But he was not paid by the railroad. Who is paying, and why?"

"Why didn't you find out when you met in Lincoln?"

"I did not know about the gold p-p-pieces until after I killed him. He said he trailed me from Trinidad, so I thought the railroad put him up to it." William just then realized the man probably had a telegram in his pocket with the name of the person he was working for on it. Next time he would turn out all the pockets.

William stared at his empty bourbon glass. The gun-fighter at Fort Sumner must have had a telegram too, but he hadn't known to look for it. Doctor Stone took his body; maybe he found it.

The thought of retracing his journey to Fort Sumner made William groan. It was time he used the telegraph to his advantage. After saying goodbye to Samuel, he strode to the telegraph office.

The clerk's eyes narrowed and his face lost color when William asked for a message form.

As William composed the message, he caught the clerk sneaking glances at him. William remembered his last visit to this office. He had threatened the clerk about keeping telegrams to would-be killers from him. Seems he laid a pretty deep track, and it took the wind a while to fill it in.

William penned his message to Doctor Stone.

Was telegram found on body of gunfighter?
Secure and Reply

William stopped. Where to have the reply sent? Here to Trinidad? He didn't want to stay in one place too long. Santa Fe? Maybe the governor could shed some light on this. Lincoln? Was he ready to get roped into that war again?

He wrote *Lincoln* and signed his name.

The next morning William bought passage for himself and Sunfish on a work train. The daily train headed to the end-of-track in the morning and returned to Trinidad at night. William shared the ride with other men heading to the construction depot. He kept Sunfish saddled and traveled with his mount in an open cattle car, stroking his horse's neck and rubbing between its ears. Along the way they passed several riders not waiting for the evening return train to Trinidad.

When the work train reached the end-of-track, William led Sunfish away from the burgeoning depot. He rode south on the graded right-of-way toward Lamy. But first he had to pass through Springer, where a riled Big Jim waited.

William rode into town, heart pounding and muscles tensed. Though nearly noon, the street held little traffic. He glanced at the stable where a knot of rope held the door closed. He wondered if Big Jim thought Doreen worth the price of a lock when morning came.

"Hey you." Big Jim strode toward him.

A gunshot echoed off the buildings, and Big Jim dove to the ground.

William threw himself from the saddle. Sunfish bolted down the street. From a low crouch, William scanned for the hidden gunman. Big Jim sprawled in the dirt, his arms crossed protectively over his head.

William sprinted for cover against the wall of the stable. A shot boomed from a cover on his right, and a spume of dirt erupted a foot to his left.

William flattened himself against the stable wall. He inched his way along until he reached the door. Yanking on the loose end of the knot freed the rope. He jerked the door open and rolled inside. Hay dust tickled his nose. He stifled a sneeze. His pulse slowed.

"Whoever you are," he shouted, "this has nothing to do with Big Jim. Hold your f-f-fire until he gets to cover."

No answer. Big Jim crawled toward the stable. The unknown gunman remained silent, out of sight.

As Big Jim pulled himself through the front door, William slipped out the back. Staying hidden as much as possible, he crept from building to building, trying the back doors. The one to the saloon was unlocked and opened into a storeroom.

He stole quietly through it and then peeked into the barroom. Only a few men occupied the main room; they crouched below the front windows.

"No shots for a time now," one man said. "Think it's safe?"

"Stand up and find out," said another.

"Wonder what that was about," the first said.

One man raised his head, then ducked like a rabbit spying a fox. "Someone's coming this way."

"Is it Big Jim?"

"Nope. A stranger."

William slid into the room behind them unnoticed

and took a seat, facing the front door with his back against the rear wall.

The lean and mustachioed man who entered through the front door looked familiar. It took a few seconds for William to place him. He was one of the two men who had hung around Trinidad with Dave Rodabaugh, leader of the gang that had thought to hire William.

Mike Roarke, he of the dry-gulch eyes.

Mike strode to the bar and ordered a whiskey, watching the front of the bar and the street beyond as he gulped it down.

William stood and kicked his chair, sending it scraping along the floor.

Mike turned at the sound and started to glance away, but then his head shot around to stare at William in shock. "Wha—?"

"Were you shooting at me, Mike?"

The others in the room scuttled out of the way in a squawking free-for-all.

Mike slowly dropped his hand so his thumb rested on the butt of his gun. "If'n I was?"

"Why?" To William, the word seemed cracked with use.

Mike relaxed his stance some. "Word come to Santa Fe you passed through Lamy. Dave and Dan rode to Trinidad, left me here in case they missed you on the back trail."

"Why does anybody care about my comings and go-ings?" William kept his eyes focused on Mike's face. "And why d-d-did you try to shoot me?"

"My own idea. I didn't want to split the money with the others."

"You do not r-r-remember me very well from Trinidad, then."

Mike nodded. "I remember you well enough. That's why I didn't want no gunfight."

William shook his head. "Fool. The money's only good if you k-k-kill me in a gunfight, in front of witnesses."

Mike's head flinched back and his eyes narrowed. "What're ya talkin' about?"

"I guess you never saw the telegram."

Mike's look of confusion deepened. "What telegram?"

A realization blossomed in William's mind. "How much money do you think you will get for k-k-killing me?"

"You know. Five twenty-dollar gold pieces."

"I think Dave has not told you the whole s-s-story."

"Thass right," said a new mushy voice from the door. "The hide of our old clown friend here is now wort' ten t'ousand."

The Return

William shifted his eyes slightly to take in the new speaker. Dan Dement stood in the doorway, leering.

"Howdy, Dan," William said. "Is Dave out there too?"

"Oh, he's around." Dan smirked.

William heard whispers jangling through the bystanders like current through a telegraph wire. "Ten thousand? For one man? Maybe we …" He saw more than one hand slide toward a holstered weapon.

Thoughts raced through his mind. He didn't want to kill anyone, but in a fraction of a second, some of the bystanders were going to draw their guns. Not to mention Dan and Mike. He needed to do something to rein it up now, and without killing anyone.

"Draw," William yelled and threw his whiskey glass

into the air, shooting the tumbling tumbler. Glass shards rained over Mike. Were Dan and Mike smart enough to see they're beaten and not go for their guns? If he cowed them, it was doubtful any of the bystanders would press the matter.

Dan clawed for his gun.

Fool, William thought and shot him. In his mind he could make a case for self-defense. He had a feeling it was increasingly important he stay on the right side of the law.

William turned his Peacemaker on Mike, who had cleared leather with his own revolver.

William shot.

Quicker than thought, death blasted Mike. He fell back, gun spinning to the floor.

William swung his revolver in a wide arc covering the bystanders, daring anyone else to draw. Hands jerked back from gun belts, and eyes dropped to stare at the floor. William backed toward the store room.

Though alive, he felt defeated. He'd hoped to handle the situation without killing, but it had gone the other way. Two more dead. And bound to get worse as the Lincoln County war escalated. A war clutching him again.

"You out there, Dave?" he yelled to the street. No answer. "I owed you four b-b-bullets from Trinidad. That was three. Got one left, just for you." William slipped out the back door.

He snuck up the alley between buildings and peered at the street. Deserted, except for Sunfish grazing at the south end of town as if never in doubt of the outcome.

Worried as to where Dave was, William hurried to Sunfish and pulled himself into the saddle. Perhaps Dave was on the way back to Santa Fe. Or Lamy. Or stalking him through the streets even now. He prodded his horse's flank with an urgent heel and left Springer.

About an hour out of town, he angled Sunfish to the southwest, intending to bypass Lamy. He set his course to Lincoln, two days' ride ahead.

He looked into the sky, shielding his eyes from the sun. It was getting hot. Where was Dave? Sweat from the heat and anxiety patterned William's back, which felt big and round like a target.

That night William picketed Sunfish and put his bedroll by a low campfire. He slept a few yards away under the cover of a bush.

He rose when the first light touched the eastern horizon. Walking a quarter mile out from his fire, he made a slow circle of the camp, looking for signs. Satisfied that no one had approached during the night, William fed Sunfish a ration of oats and ate a hard biscuit for breakfast. Then he swung into the saddle and put Sunfish into a trot toward Lincoln.

All day he rode, periodically altering the gait from trot to walk. He wanted to make the best time possible, but arrive with a horse fresh enough for trouble. He drew near to Lincoln in the late afternoon.

He heard the town before he saw it. The wind carried gunshots from Lincoln.

Approaching from the northwest, the Dolan side of town was nearest. William dismounted and edged in for a closer look.

Gunmen held the McSween house under siege. Men, fanned out in every building across the street, poured shots into the adobe structure. Riding down the street would be suicide. And to get to the beleaguered McSweens, he'd have to ride openly past Murphy's headquarters. The narrow width of the valley where the town sat made it impossible to ride around without going miles out of the way.

William took his rifle from the sling and with a slap on Sunfish's flank sent his horse away. He picked his way from cover to cover along the rear of the buildings, heading to the corral behind the neighboring Tunstall store. Hearing people in the McSween house return fire reminded him he did not have time to waste. He hurried along with less caution.

Soldiers held the corral.

William stopped moving. The soldiers, their attention directed to the back of the house, did not see him. Their rifles pointed at the back veranda, but they were not firing. William scratched his chin in understanding. They were making sure no one escaped out the back this time, like they think Billy did before.

A corporal led the squad of ten soldiers. A fat corporal.

One twitch of his internal tornado and William found himself standing in plain view, rifle in his left hand.

"What are you doing here, c-co-corporal?" William asked loud enough to be heard over the gunfire. "No Indians in there."

The fat biscuit in a soldier suit whipped around, pop-eyed. "You? What are you doing here?" Then he composed himself. "Well, well, this is my lucky day."

"I asked what *you* are doing here. This cannot be legitimate army b-b-business."

The corporal gave a sly smile and shrugged. "Orders from the colonel. I hope you plan to interfere."

"And if I do?"

The corporal looked around at the other soldiers who no longer watched the house but looked at one another with uncertainty. "Ten against one."

In a glance, William measured the other soldiers. Half of them slouched, looked away, or stood locked in place, uneasy about backing the corporal. Once again that fat fool had misjudged the situation. And him. The corporal's outright fouling of William's gun at the gunfight with Torrey amounted to attempted murder. Not something William would let slide.

"Tell your men to stand d-do-down. Or I will settle with you for the good c-c-care you took of my guns in Fort Sumner." He tried to keep ice in his voice, but the heat of anger turned it into a growl. "Hoot."

"A clown to the end. Shoot him, men," the corporal said, reaching for his sidearm.

William shouldn't kill him. The thought intertwined with another. He was going to enjoy this. The corporal was nothing, a bag of bluster held up by a uniform. But it was an army uniform. A tightening of his throat thrilled a warning against starting a shooting war with the army.

William's revolver glided out of its holster as the corporal's hand touched his own pistol. He hoped the soldiers realized it was not the uniform he disrespected.

William shot the fat corporal twice, once through each suspender.

The soldiers stood wide-eyed in shock.

Then a fusillade of shots between the house and the street broke the spell.

"Stand down," William said to the soldiers. "If you are really here on Colonel Dudley's orders, break up this gunfight instead of s-s-supporting it. Sort it all out legally."

But one of the soldiers blinked away his confusion and shouted, "He killed Corporal O'Rourke." He leveled his rifle at William.

Though five of the soldiers snorted in derision, three others brought their rifles to bear on William.

He refused to kill any of these men. They didn't look none too steady. William shot over their heads, and when they ducked in reflex, he ran for cover. He saw the Torreón just ahead and dove through its small door. Wild rifle shots chased him as he slammed it shut.

William peered through the small firing slit in the door. The soldiers had abandoned their watch of the back of the house and were fanning out to fire at the Torreón. He settled back on his heels and sighed. He didn't fancy shooting it out with soldiers, didn't want to fire on the army at all, except that fat corporal. But he had cleared the way for escape by those trapped in the McSween house. He needed to keep the soldiers busy and hoped he could do so without killing anyone else.

This probably tore it with staying on the right side of the law. He pegged a few shots with his rifle, kicking up dust and stone chips, making the soldiers pull their heads in.

Now with the door closed, he found a stout wooden beam that had been leaning against the wall behind it. He dropped the bar into braces on the door frame and secured the Torreón.

William climbed the stairs to the second floor. He had a clear view of the soldiers' positions. Only four fired at the tower. The other five sat to their rear, loading their rifles or unpacking ammunition. He studied their supplies; the only thing that would threaten his position was dynamite. He didn't see any. There was some in the Tunstall store, and Dolan undoubtedly had a supply, but for now the soldiers lacked the means to take the tower.

William scooted to his left until he saw the front of the Tunstall store through a firing slit. The McSween house was just beyond, and the men who besieged it were well hidden.

It looked bad. At least twenty guns fired into the adobe-and-wood structure, and a fog of gun smoke hid the upper street and the Dolan House from view. Tactically he had little advantage and could offer no aid to the defenders. However, if any of the gunmen stepped into the street, they would be easy targets.

As if on signal, the hail of bullets from the besiegers ceased. A voice shouted over the sporadic fire still coming from the house. Jesse's voice.

"Billy, enough of this. Surrender—and come out with your hands up."

What? Billy was still in town? The young outlaw had been wounded weeks before. Perhaps he had left and returned, at which time Dolan's men struck.

A voice from the house called back. But it wasn't Billy's voice; it was Alex McSween.

"My wife's in here. Hold your fire and let her come out."

"Sure," Jesse called. "Anyone who wants to come out, come on. Hands in the air, and no guns."

From his angle, William could not see the front of the house. He guessed from the relaxing postures of the men that someone had emerged. In a moment a figure hove into his line of sight; Susan McSween stared down the men who were attacking her home.

Jesse stepped from cover, his gun pointed at the ground.

For a moment a tornado roiled in his mind. William grasped the edge of the gun slit to keep from losing control. McSween's wife was in jeopardy. A dark, twisted part of him wanted to shoot Jesse like a clay pigeon, but he refused to give in.

The truce was not his to break and Susan's life was forfeit if he did. William stared through the sights of his rifle at Jesse, though he did not remember even aiming the gun. He eased his finger off the trigger.

"Just you?" Jesse asked. "No one else in the house wants to come out?"

"I saw soldiers," Susan said. "I'll have the army put a stop to this."

Jesse laughed. "You'll find them right up the street there," he said, pointing past the Torreón. "I'm sure you'll find Colonel Dudley most accommodating."

Men Shall Burn

Colonel Dudley—here? William scurried to the other side of the tower and looked up the street to the east end of town.

A half mile away hunkered an entire troop of fifty soldiers blocking the road.

Susan hiked her skirts above her ankles and ran toward them.

William shifted and took stock of the soldiers laying siege to the tower. Their positions had not changed and no reinforcements had come. It looked like the army was here in support and that the colonel might not take an otherwise active role. He was merely to provide the corks for the kill jar and let Dolan work uninterrupted. The town boss was holding nothing back; this was the big push—all or nothing.

Dread for the men still in the McSween house boiled through William like a thunderhead. He wondered if they knew they were doomed. As if in answer to his thoughts, guns opened up on the house again. When William returned to the position overlooking the street, Jesse was gone.

William knew the besiegers were not aware of his position, but as soon as he fired, his advantage of surprise would be lost. There was little he could do to save the men in the house. But if he could get Jesse, it might be enough to break up the assault. Lining up his rifle sights on Jesse's last position, William waited.

A loud thump on the door of the Torreón reverberated up the stairs. William ran to check. Two soldiers had charged the door and were battering it with their shoulders. But he couldn't get the rifle at an acute enough angle through the gun slit to stop them.

He vaulted down the stairs and looked through the slit in the wooden door. The two soldiers now stood a foot away, rubbing their shoulders. They looked perplexed, undecided.

William made up their minds for them. He shot a couple of rounds through the firing slit, aiming wide.

The soldiers scattered and scrambled back to cover. A hail of shots from the others peppered the thick mud walls of the tower.

William fired wide again, kicking up dirt and sending bullets whining over the soldiers' heads. How long before they get the rest of the troop involved? He might have to shoot in earnest. It could be a long siege. Maybe they thought they could run him out of ammunition.

He stopped firing and searched for a marked spot in the dirt floor near the curved wall. Digging down a few inches, he brought out the cache of bullets he had stored there weeks before. With a grim smile, he knew he could last longer than the soldiers expected.

After plinking a few more shots out the door slit, he raced upstairs where the angle of fire was better. The soldiers' firing now was more sporadic, and William returned one shot per five. He was safe for the moment—though his heart strained at being holed up and out of the fight.

What had Susan accomplished with Colonel Dudley? The army had not made any effort to stop the battle at the McSween home, but neither had they given it further support. His mind ran first one way and then another, like a hungry coyote raiding a town of prairie dogs, but couldn't catch a single idea.

The night was difficult. Firing continued intermittently at the house, and though the soldiers watching the tower stopped shooting at sundown, William did not trust himself to sleep. He peered out at the corral below, wondering why the rest of the troop had not joined in the assault.

Then flames burst from the McSween house. Fiery tongues shot into the air, illuminating a greasy smoke. The air blowing through William's gun ports grew hot. Shouts from Dolan's men and screams from the burning house split the night. The men in the street continued shooting into the burning house; the returned shots grew less frequent, then stopped altogether.

The house burned through the night, until it collapsed with a great eruption of sparks and flung embers.

By morning, the army was gone.

William stayed in the Torreón until midmorning, just to be sure. He itched to find out what had happened to his friends at the McSween house but forced himself to wait. He stared so hard at the smoking ruin that his eyes burned. Worse, there were bodies stretched in the road in front of the house's smoldering skeleton. Were his friends dead? If they were, getting himself killed wouldn't help. William paced around the top of the tower, more restless than any undead spirit.

When he could stand it no longer, William unbarred the door and left the Torreón. No one opposed him. He hurried to the ruins of the McSween home.

Charred timbers stuck out at sharp angles, and the stone chimney pointed an accusing finger at the sky. Acrid smoke filled his nostrils, and some of the adobe clinkers still glowed hot.

The bodies were gone. William met hostile glares all around. He wondered where Jesse was. This was the perfect time for that 'gunfight in front of witnesses.' He carried his rifle with his left hand curled around the firing chamber and barrel pointed down, but kept his right hand free and ready to draw. His mind locked, he moved by instinct. He felt like a tree waving in a wind at the edge of a coming storm.

He stood in front of the Dolan House and stared at the door without memory of walking there. It could be death to enter, but he had to know. After a moment, William laid his rifle against the front steps and ascended.

Dolan sat in an overstuffed chair in the entrance hall. A gunman stood by his right side, fingers twitching. No Jesse.

"I wondered if you were coming in or not," Dolan said. A sling cradled his right arm.

William stared at him in silence, afraid to ask about the bodies.

"Are ye looking for work?" Dolan asked. "I could use a good gun hand like you. Me forces have been … depleted … of late. Or do you consider yourself still employed by … well, the other side?"

William gave a brief shake of his head, his eyes returning to the gunman by Dolan's side. "Who is left?"

Dolan leaned back into the cushions of the armchair, a smile spreading a twinkle to his eye. "Let's see. . . . Brewer was killed in a gunfight a couple of days ago. We got Alex McSween and five Regulators last night. . . . Not many left I think."

A heavy weight landed on William's heart. Alex—dead? "Hoot, hoot." Was it true? It could be a trick. He wouldn't believe it until he saw for himself. "I want to see McSween's body."

Dolan waved his hand as if chasing away a gnat. "So as I see it . . . if ye want to keep working in Lincoln . . . ye work for me."

"What about Billy? Is he d-d-dead too?"

A scowl replaced Dolan's smile. "Got away in the fire. Ducked out the back. I'd say he had the luck o' the Irish, if I wasn't blasphemin' to say it."

William took a deep breath. So he had done some good after all. He gathered his wits. "Where's Jesse?"

"Still working for me. I sent him on an errand this morning." Dolan furrowed his brow, studying William. "Not finished with him yet, are ye? Too bad, I'd love to have ye working for me. But . . . well, not yet, I think."

"Not ever," William said, and turned slightly to face down the gun hand standing beside Dolan. "But I will w-w-wait for Jesse's return."

"Not so fast," Dolan said. "Ye got a telegram yesterday,

but we didn't know ye were back in town, so I held onto it. I think you'll leave Lincoln when ye read it."

Dolan rose from his chair with a grimace and limped to the telegraph in the corner. He pulled open a drawer, took out a crumpled telegram, and handed it to William.

TELEGRAM FOUND ON BODY. DUDLEY TOOK IT.
DR. STONE

"Seems ye got business in Fort Sumner."

William stood undecided, studying Dolan's face. "What do you know about the Fort Sumner telegram?"

"Nothing. Jesse thought it important so I sent him to fetch it."

"Then I will just wait here in Lincoln for him to bring it."

A smile curled Dolan's lip. "From what he tells me, that would suit him just fine. He said if you were to show up to keep you here, unharmed, until he got back."

"So why tell me to g-go to Fort Sumner?"

"It's inconvenient to me for you to be in town just now. Unless you're working for me, that is. I'm taking over the Tunstall store."

Anger knotting within him gave William's vision red edges. He took a deep breath and then asked, "Did you forget about Susan McSween? What w-w-will she say about losing the store?" The fact of Alex's death burrowed in like a tick. "Do you think she would sell to you after you k-k-killed her husband?"

"Mrs. McSween left for Fort Sumner this morning with the soldiers. I'm sure she and I will strike some sort of bargain. After all, without her husband, what other choice does she have?"

For a moment, William considered shooting the gunman, and then turning his revolver on the wounded Dolan. Alex, John, Brewer, even Emily, cried out to him for vengeance. Jesse was the venom, but this was the spider behind the web.

So easy to kill them all, then lie in wait for Jesse's return and take him too. At least three more killings—some of them murders. Bile rose in William's throat. What was he thinking? Was his soul that corrupt?

"I think I had better r-r-ride to Fort Sumner. If I can find my horse."

Sunfish, still saddled, stood picking through the hay in the corral behind the Tunstall store. The horse was skittish so near to the smoldering ruins of the McSween house, but had returned nevertheless to this familiar place.

While tending to his horse, William thought about his skirmish with the soldiers. He had killed a corporal of the US Army. How safe would he be at Fort Sumner? Returning there was dangerous, but he sensed that the corporal had not been well liked by his men. As to an official response, Dudley had twenty thousand reasons to keep William free. It might be enough.

William rode away from Lincoln at the hottest time of the day. He knew Jesse had a six-hour head start. He didn't want to stumble on his adversary's camp, and took the chance the outlaw would hurry to Fort Sumner, perhaps even ride through the night. Just as well, for there was no purpose running into Jesse before he retrieved the telegram.

But what about when Jesse was on the way back to Lincoln, telegram in hand? Yes; two birds with one stone.

William scrutinized the landscape. He wanted a spot at least a half day's ride from Lincoln, with good cover along a narrowing in the road. He did not plan to shoot from ambush, but wanted Jesse within revolver range before he revealed himself.

The uncooperative terrain revealed only an undulating panorama of open space punctuated with a scattering of short trees. A man's camp would be visible for miles in such country.

The telegraph wires, marching along on poles like giant storks wading across the landscape, marked the most direct line from Lincoln to Fort Sumner. But the wires scaled cliffs and forded rivers while men must detour around such inconveniences of geography.

The road took a more meandering course, for the traveler had one need that the telegraph did not. Water. Horses, whether of the iron or the blood-and-bone type, depended on it.

William knew of a watering hole. It was closer to Fort Sumner than Lincoln, and if Jesse rode quickly, he would pass it on his return before William was ready. In that case, they would run into each other on the open road. Not ideal, but not the ruination of his plan either.

Night fell and William made a quick camp along the trail. He figured Jesse, if riding hard, would only now be arriving in Fort Sumner. Even if Dudley gave up the telegram without delay, the outlaw couldn't get this far by morning.

Up with the sun, William rode with his hat brim pulled low against the glare. What if Jesse guessed the plan and got to the spring before him? Then he'd be riding into Jesse's gun. William urged Sunfish faster. The telegraph poles paralleled the road for some distance but then swung away. He met a few riders going toward Lincoln who pulled up to look at him wide-eyed and open-mouthed as he rode past, for he did not stop to talk.

Sunfish wheezed and his flanks ran with sweat by the time William reached the watering hole, a freshet of a spring that filled a small pool surrounded by live oak.

The quiet pool lay a few yards off the road. William dismounted and stole in. No sign of another camp, no sign of Jesse. William let out a deep breath. Sunfish was spent, but he had arrived first.

Contemplations by a Quiet Pool

After unsaddling his horse, William let Sunfish drink and rest in the shade. He examined the ground between the road and the pool. Horse tracks dimpled the area, but the churned earth in all of them except those left by Sunfish lay dried by the sun.

With a pine branch William swept the area clear of prints. There wasn't much cover, but he stretched out by the pool and waited. Farther to the south he saw the faint line the telegraph drew across the sun-branded land. The heat made his eyelids heavy. Flies buzzing around his ears kept him awake. The odor of fresh manure stung his nostrils. He looked over at Sunfish, who rolled his eyes and shook his head.

The day died with the sun flame red in the west. The deepening sky birthed a sickle-thin infant moon.

Jesse did not come that night or the next day. Or the day after that. No riders traveled the road in either direction. William scanned the horizons for sign of a storm. The wind felt electric, but he saw no dark clouds. The air hung like a breath of suspense.

During the long hours of waiting, thoughts piled in his mind like distant clouds. He remembered Emily and wondered if she was back in England. He thought of John and Alex. What did he owe the dead?

Alone, left to wrestle with his inner demons without guidance, he remembered a Bible story about Jesus wrestling with the devil in the wilderness. William laughed, for he had water, food, and a horse. Some wilderness. Jesus had wrestled with bigger problems than his; this was enough of a wilderness for him.

Would killing Jesse be enough? Should he also kill Dolan? His dreams of settling in Lincoln were lost whatever he did.

He thought of Susan and contemplated his own future. Would his body, his spirit already long crushed by loneliness, plod along step by hopeless step until he dropped on some dirty street, left to be consumed by dogs? Who could ever love a killer like him?

He didn't want to kill Jesse, but neither did he want the man to go unpunished for the bad things that he'd done. However, ruining William's life was not one of them. Jesse might have put the first gun in William's hand, but like being tempted by the devil, he himself had taken it from there.

With a start, William realized that he chose the water hole to confront Jesse because he didn't really want to kill the man. The unspoken custom of necessity that made a water hole neutral, nearly sacred, territory reined up the impulse to shoot first and ask questions later. At this point Jesse was a means to an end. The telegram and the people behind the price on his head. That's all Jesse meant to him now.

He was done with Lincoln and all its killing. He resolved to never kill again, *unless* he absolutely had to. He wanted to settle with whoever put a price on his head. Once that was done, he would take off his guns.

That thought brought some comfort, but was it correct? He set up a test. If Jesse arrived at the watering hole before the next day, it meant God approved.

The storm William expected stayed beyond the horizon. He ate the last of his rations for supper. He slept, trusting to Sunfish to wake him if a rider approached.

The next morning, no Jesse. William kicked at his bedroll. To hell with the test. He saddled his horse and rode toward Fort Sumner.

He had been riding for forty-five minutes when the road curved and the line of telegraph poles once again ran alongside. As William passed the junction, he noted that a narrow trail had been beaten out underneath the telegraph line—for work crews to maintain the wire, he imagined. But then he saw a curious print in the newly exposed soil.

He swung down from Sunfish to get a better look. Among the crushed blades of grass a hoofprint was stamped into a patch of bare ground. A horse had recently been ridden down the work trail—a horse that had the letter *J* filed into one of its shoes.

His rations spent, he needed to resupply at Fort Sumner, so he could not follow Jesse down this narrow path. He had missed his chance at the telegram Jesse carried. Damn the luck. William climbed onto his horse and rode on.

He approached Fort Sumner sitting tall in the saddle, eyes darting about, prepared to gallop away if he saw more than five soldiers on the street, or if any group of more than two soldiers showed interest in him.

Unless he could get the name on the telegram, he couldn't go forward. Colonel Dudley had the name, but was it safe to go on the post? Maybe McAdams could help.

Seeing nothing to alarm him, he went to Marshal McAdams's office. The office was unoccupied, the cells in the back empty. William pulled a chair around so he could watch the street through the window and waited.

William hoped that McAdams knew the name, but if not, then perhaps he would intercede with Dudley. The colonel wanted something in return, and William did not have anything close to the twenty thousand dollars Dudley demanded.

William's reverie broke when he saw McAdams walking down the street. The marshal stopped to examine William's horse and glanced at the door to the office. He rubbed a hand over his brow and entered.

"Howdy, William. Back again?"

William rose from his chair, his mouth tightened into a wince of a smile. "I hope that is not a problem."

McAdams returned William's tentative smile with a shrug. "Have you been to Lincoln recently?"

"A few days ago."

McAdams locked eyes with him. "Before or after the McSween house burned down?"

William let out a deep breath. "During."

McAdams nodded. "Heard a rumor you were there and that you killed Corporal O'Rourke. Is that true?"

"It is. What are they s-s-saying about me? Am I w-w-wanted by the army?"

"No. It's just a story making the rounds with the beer. Some say O'Rourke got what he deserved. You shooting O'Rourke is more of an embellishment; Lincoln is the main topic."

McAdams walked to the stove and picked up the coffeepot. He motioned with it toward William, eyebrows raised.

William shook his head. "What are they saying about Lincoln?"

"If you listen to the stories, you'd believe Lincoln is a ghost town now—burned out. But Susan McSween came back with Dudley and she told me what really happened." McAdams poured a cup of coffee and sat at his desk.

William sat down and steepled his fingers under his chin. "I am glad she made it here s-s-safely. The last I saw of her she was going to talk to the soldiers in Lincoln. I worried because she did not know they were there in support of Dolan."

"She found that out. Begged Colonel Dudley to help. He did nothing. But at least when her husband, Alex, was killed, the colonel offered to give her safe conduct back here."

William stared at the floor. "They killed Alex, and I could do nothing to stop them. How is Mrs. McSween?"

"Grieving, but busy as a hornet smoked from her nest. She's been firing up the telegraph. Sent appeals to Washington. Even one direct to President Hayes."

"What good will that do?"

McAdams took a long pull from his coffee cup and then set it on his desk. "The law, US government law, is coming. To the north, Colorado's been a state for two years already. The days of the wide-open West as a territory are coming to an end. Maybe this mess in Lincoln will bring the end a little sooner."

"What happens to you?" William asked. "Will you not be out of a job?"

"We'll have to make the transition, you and I. For me, I could still be a federal marshal, with better pay and more deputies. For you ..." McAdams picked up his coffee cup, took a loud sip. "Gunfighters are a dying breed."

"Always have been." Another reason to hang up his guns, but not until this mess with Jesse and Washburn was finished. "I do not plan to stay too long in town, Marshal. But I need some information from Colonel Dudley, and I am not sure if it is safe to go see him."

"You're not a wanted man as far as I know. But once you're on the post, I have no jurisdiction and you're on your own."

William stared at McAdams. The marshal was on the side of the law. Did he know about the telegrams urging people to kill William? What would the marshal do if he did know?

The lawman sat unperturbed under William's scrutiny.

"Marshal," William said at last, "I could use your help."

McAdams listened quietly as William explained. When he finished, the marshal rose from his chair and paced.

"I knew the gunfighter you faced at the fort said he was to be paid ten thousand dollars, but I had no idea someone from back east had loosed a flood of them at you. It's against the law to put out private contracts on people. I'll help you put a stop to it." McAdams continued to pace. "Obviously it has something to do with that reporter Washburn who was killed back in Trinidad. But what?"

William tapped his shirt three times. "That is why I need to see the t-t-telegram so I can find out who it is that wants to know when I am killed. Hoot. And Colonel Dudley saw the telegram, though he might have given it to Jesse."

"I could ask Dudley," McAdams said, "but I've no jurisdiction on the post and can't force him to tell me."

"He probably will not tell you anyway, because he hopes to sell me the information."

"If he gave the telegram to Jesse, then there's nothing in his office that'll help us."

Warmth blossomed in William's chest as he noted the marshal had said help *us.* "Before we give up, is there some way to find out if he really did give the telegram to Jesse?"

"Anything Dudley says is suspect. We'd have to look around his office and hope we find it. Or, we can do what Dudley wants and buy it from him."

William sighed. "His price is twenty thousand dollars."

McAdams's eyes widened. "That crooked bastard."

William nodded and smiled. "That is what I thought."

McAdams's brow furrowed and he stared out the window. "I'll ask Dudley to come to my office and then I'll question him about the telegram."

"But you said we cannot trust anything he says—"

"I don't expect he'll tell me anything. But while I have him here, you sneak into his office and have a look around."

"Why, Marshal, are you suggesting I b-b-break the law?"

"I didn't say you should take anything. Just find the telegram if it's there and read it."

"That is still breaking and entering."

"Not if you find an open window and don't take anything. Then it's just trespassing. Not enough of a law break to bother me."

"If I get caught poking around on a military post, I could be charged with spying."

"Don't get caught."

Safe as a Hen's Egg in a Stampede

William said, "I will try my b-b-best. I doubt Colonel Dudley gave the telegram to Jesse. Why would he if he h-h-hopes to sell it to me? But if I am about to be caught, I will shoot my way out, and count on your cooperation in getting away."

"I don't know about that." Marshal McAdams sighed. "But for now, put your horse in the stable. Let's not advertise that you're in town."

Doctor Stone's face popped into William's mind. "Wait, Marshal." William swiveled his chair. "Before we do this, there is one other p-p-person to see—someone on our side. Doctor Stone."

"Has he seen the telegram?"

"Maybe. Or he could know if Dudley still has it. Or

perhaps he would have a b-be-better chance to get a look at it."

McAdams rapped on his desk. "Sounds like a better idea. I'll ask the doc to come here for a chat. Should be less difficult than getting Dudley to come at that. You stay out of sight. I'll drop your horse at the stable on the way."

"Thanks. Say hello to Emmett for me."

William watched McAdams leave the office and un-loop Sunfish's reins from the hitching post. The horse gave a toss of its head and turned to look at William through the office window. William rapped his knuckles on the glass. Sunfish chuffed and followed the marshal toward the stable.

William sat down to wait. He wondered if Alex McSween's body would be brought to Fort Sumner for burial. Who would come to the funeral? How many of the Regulators were left? And what of Alex's wife, Susan? The McSweens had come from Kansas—would she return there? Go home like Emily did?

He didn't have many chips left in this game. Just one last hand with Jesse.

McAdams returned with Doctor Stone.

"William." The physician stuck out his hand. "Glad to see you again."

William stood and shook it. "Thanks for answering my telegram." Feeling nervous, he rapped on the desk three times. "You said Dudley took the gunfighter's telegram. Did you r-r-read it before he did?"

"I glanced at it. I was looking for something with the gunfighter's name on it, so I could properly fill out the death certificate. His name wasn't there, so I tossed it aside." The doctor sighed. "The colonel came to my office later, wanting to know more about the man. He saw the telegram and took it. I didn't think it was important. Sorry."

"Do you remember who the telegram was from?" McAdams asked. "Any contact information?"

"Some law firm in Massachusetts. Don't remember where."

William slumped back into his chair. "Hooty hoot."

"I do have some good news, though, William," Doctor Stone said. "I've been thinking about your illness."

William looked up at Stone's earnest face. He remembered the quiet pool where he had waited for Jesse and his decision to not let his condition control his life. "So have I."

Stone continued, his triumphant smile leaving no room to register William's comment. "I can finally recommend a treatment. I discussed the matter with some of my colleagues from back east—marvelous invention the telegraph—it will revolutionize medicine. We agreed a nerve tonic is indicated."

"A nerve tonic?" William sniffed. "There is nothing

wrong with my nerves. If anything, my nerves are too s-s-strong." His left hand shot out to strike the table.

"Exactly. This tonic will put them back in balance. Slow them down if you like."

"Sounds like it could g-g-get me killed."

"Nonsense. It's made from sassafras and cocaine. Very soothing for the nerves. I'll mix you up a bottle."

Now William was sure it would get him killed.

"Thanks, Doc," William said. "I will think about it." He looked out the window. "In the meanwhile, I still have to p-p-put a stop to this telegram business. Medicine is not the only thing those electrified wires have revolutionized. Used to be I could ride far enough that trouble got left behind. Now I have to get beyond the end of the wire to be safe." He turned back to the doctor. "I need to see that telegram."

"Maybe Colonel Dudley will show it to you," Doctor Stone said.

"Does he still have it?"

"I assume so. Why wouldn't he?"

"Dolan sent Jesse Evans to f-f-fetch it. I know Jesse is on his way back to Lincoln. Maybe with the telegram?"

Doctor Stone shrugged.

"Back to our first plan, then?" McAdams asked.

Doctor Stone's eyebrows arched. "First plan?"

"Looking for the telegram in Dudley's office," McAdams said.

"Why not just ask him?"

"He offered to s-s-sell it, or at least the information I need, to me. For twenty thousand dollars."

Doctor Stone shook his head. "That crooked bastard."

William and McAdams shot each other a smile. "That's what w-w-we thought."

"I'm willing to help," Doctor Stone said. "What can I do?"

*　　*　　*

Later that afternoon, Doctor Stone walked William through the fort's gate and into his medical office. To hide the tics, Stone had draped one of William's arms over his shoulders and supported him at the waist as William hobbled like an injured man, his head low.

Safely in the office, Stone smashed the glass on his medicine cabinet and scattered some papers around the floor.

"Vandals," Doctor Stone said. "I'll go for Colonel Dudley so he can see the damage for himself. I'll try to get him to bring his aide along, but you'd better get into his office through the window and not risk being seen. I estimate you'll have no more than five minutes to look around."

"Thanks, Doc."

William climbed out the window at the back of Stone's office. He slipped along the rear of the row of buildings, ducking under each window until he reached the corner of the parade quadrangle. He bit down on the inside of his cheek and crossed the open space, trying to stroll, but his insides were taut as a wire.

Reaching the back of the army headquarters building, William crouched beside Dudley's window, which was open to catch the breeze. He waited, listening.

He heard Doctor Stone rush into the colonel's office and report the ransacking of his dispensary.

Colonel Dudley strode from his office, calling for his aide.

So far, so good. William had five minutes. He climbed through the window.

William stepped to the colonel's desk. The last time he had seen Dudley with a telegram, it had just been lying there in the open. Now the objects on the polished mahogany lay as neatly ordered as a battlefield before the mayhem. No telegrams.

He pulled open the top drawer. Folders stuffed inches thick with papers filled it. William's fingers turned them like a plow while he scanned the labels. Nothing. One minute gone.

The side drawer was locked. He hesitated; forcing it would be breaking and entering. More important, a broken lock would tip Dudley someone had been here. With other places to look, he'd leave this locked drawer for last and hope there was no need to break it open. He moved to a cabinet against the wall. Two minutes gone. The colonel must be in Stone's office by now.

William rifled through the papers and books in the cabinet. Nothing looked promising. Where would Dudley keep a telegram—something the crooked army officer thought he could sell for twenty thousand dollars? Somewhere safe.

An inspiration hit him and he whirled to look into the rear corner of the office. An iron safe squatted there, as unassailable as a miser's heart. Shit. "Hoot. Hoot, hooty hoot." Three minutes gone.

The colonel's door flew open. His aide stood there, pistol leveled at William's chest. "Stand still. Hands up. What are you doing here?"

Time slowed. William bit back on the rising storm within. He had told McAdams he would shoot his way out if caught, but then what? He raised his hands.

"Take your guns out slowly and put them on the desk," the aide, a sergeant, said with a sweeping motion of his pistol.

William complied. He didn't feel unarmed as long as his guns were within reach, though an icy memory sliced through his mind. He'd thought the same thing the last time they disarmed him in this very office. He'd barely talked his way out of that. And this was worse.

His palms itched. He longed to grab his guns and run, but tension held him rigid. Heavy footfalls echoed in the outer office. Now or never.

Colonel Dudley strode into the office, trailed by Doctor Stone.

William let out a deep sigh. He'd planned to hang up his guns when this was over, so maybe this was for the best. He turned his attention from his guns and looked Dudley in the eye. "Hello, Colonel."

"Is this our vandal?" Dudley said to Doctor Stone. Turning to William, he smiled, his mouth a crooked line. "Looking for this, perhaps?" He pulled a folded paper from an inside pocket of his uniform. "When I sent Jesse away without it, I figured you'd be after it sooner or later."

Gorge rose in William's throat. The telegram was right there. He could kill both the colonel and his sergeant and be gone. He closed his eyes. After a few deep breaths, he said, "You can keep it." His life and the damned telegram.

"I believe I shall," Dudley said, and slipped the paper back into his tunic. "In the meantime, enjoy the hospitality of federal prison. Sergeant, lock him up."

"On what charge?" Doctor Stone asked. "He hasn't stolen anything."

"Trespassing, Doctor. Maybe I'll throw in a charge of spying. I can hang him for that."

Doctor Stone's face went white. "You wouldn't."

The sergeant motioned for William to lead the way.

William moved through the door.

Colonel Dudley called after him. "Of course, it may all be a misunderstanding. I could look the other way, drop the charges. The cost is thirty thousand dollars. And to show there are no hard feelings, I'll even throw in the telegram."

William wished he'd shot him.

Dinner with Rats

This time the sergeant did not take William to the bachelor officers' quarters, but to the fort's jail. The stifling cells stank of stale urine and moldy bread. Air circulated through a small barred rectangle in the heavy wooden door and a strip of a window high on the opposite wall. The corners lay in deep shadow. The bedding on the cot shivered with vermin.

William sat with his back to the wall, legs stretched out before him. Had he been going about things all wrong? If federal prison was anything like this, he'd rather be hanged.

Thirty thousand dollars would make it all go away. Dudley must be crazy to ask for such an absurd amount of money. William had no way to raise anything like that, so buying his way free was impossible. Maybe McAdams or Stone could break him out. A marshal and a doctor? He snorted in derision for grasping at such straws. At least they knew where he was. He would be in real trouble if Dudley tried to move him to some secret location. His only hope was to stay in touch with Doctor Stone and wait for some chance of rescue to come along.

If he gave up gunfighting, his illness put him at the mercy of others and he hated that. Powerlessness, more disturbing than Indians on the horizon, flowed through him. He concentrated on his breathing. Let it go. Let it be. Wait, bide your time. He touched each button on his shirt three times in cadence with his thoughts.

A soldier shoved a tin plate of greasy slop through a slot in the door, then slammed the cover. William tasted the runny gruel; someone was starving a pig today. He set the plate in a dark corner by the urine pail.

As the dark hours passed, William schemed. Thirty thousand dollars was a prodigious amount, more than a cattleman like Tunstall had paid all his ranch hands together in a year. William counted his assets—a dark cell and three friends. No matter which way he plowed the furrows, he didn't have enough seed.

His thoughts drifted to his slain friend. John Tunstall had a dark side to mirror William's own. Had the friendship that developed between them been just one blotted soul recognizing another? And Tunstall's depravity had contaminated Emily. Or had a hidden shadow lurked in Emily's heart too?

Left hand, right hand, William tom-tommed his fingers on his forehead. The preacher of his childhood had said it took solid character to survive in the West, a forge that broke you if the steel of your soul harbored flaws. Tunstall was dead; Emily returned home in failure. And he was a killer, the most flawed of all.

Would he survive the forge? Left hand, right hand. His father had told him that his illness was a sign of tainted character. If so, he was sure to break. Might he go mad? Try to hang himself?

Left hand, right hand, then back to touching his shirt buttons.

Rats crawled into his cell that night. William shivered in revulsion when one scurried across his legs. The tin plate with the uneaten meal scraped as something pushed it along the floor in the shadows. More than one rat? William clasped his knees to his chest, thankful that the soldiers had left him his clothes—and his boots. He'd heard tales of men tossed naked into the dark cells.

Sometimes they were no longer men when they were released.

William got to his feet and crouched in a corner. Stomping the rats if they came for him was his only defense.

His belly growled. He wondered what rat tasted like. And who was hungrier, him or them?

Metal banging against the bars woke him. In the shadowy cell, William couldn't tell the time—only that a strip of daylight filtered through the high-set window. Hunger chawed at his middle, and thirst parched his thought.

Colonel Dudley and three soldiers stared through the barred cell-door window.

"You've had some time to think it over," Dudley said. "Do we have a deal?"

"I do not have thirty thousand d-d-dollars. And while locked in here, no chance to get it."

Dudley pushed his face closer to the opening so that his fleshy nose squeezed between two bars. "So if I let you out, you *will* get it?"

"I have no way to raise that much money."

Dudley stepped back. "Mull it over some more. I haven't filed the spying charges yet. I'll give you until tomorrow morning to think of something."

William grunted, shrugged his shoulders, and turned away.

Dudley blew out an exasperated breath. "You're not trying hard enough."

William sat back against the far wall, legs outstretched again.

Dudley leaned close to whisper through the bars. "Ask Mrs. McSween for the money, fool. I'll make arrangements for you to see her today."

"I would never ask her," William said. "Even if she had that much."

"She'll have it once Dolan buys out her interest in the Tunstall store." Dudley stepped back. "I'll be back for your answer tomorrow morning."

The four men shuffled away, leaving William to ponder this newest cruelty.

Raising a false hope of succor, offering vinegar to a man dying of thirst. Why would Dolan pay Alex's widow that much for property she had to abandon anyway? And if he did, why would she give her future security to William? They were not that close. But even if they were that close, he'd never ask her to give up Alex's legacy for his own sake.

William's resolve weakened as the day wore on and he faced another hungry night in the rat-infested cell. He heard footsteps in the hall, and he turned away from the door. Then the welcome sound of a key turning in the lock brought him around.

Susan McSween stood in the doorway, a canteen slung over her shoulder and a basket in her hand. Though two guards stood behind her, William ignored them in favor of the aroma of beans and bacon.

"Colonel Dudley let me bring you some supper." Susan handed him the canteen. She put the basket on the floor. "I'm afraid it's just some beans, but I hope it'll do."

William drank three long draughts from the canteen. His body wanted more, but he forced himself to stop. "Thank you." He turned to the basket. "Beans are a banquet to a starving man."

"Marshal McAdams told me the colonel had you locked up, but Dudley wouldn't let me see you. Then this afternoon the colonel tells me to bring you supper."

William nodded, salivating. "Have you eaten yet? Care to join me?"

Susan laughed. "No, go right ahead. I'm just glad to see you're not hurt."

William attacked the bowl of beans—a tactical error on Dudley's part, for with food and water came renewed resolve and strength.

"Dudley said you wanted to ask me something."

So that's it. He wants him to ask her for money. "There *is* something I want to ask you," William said. "I am so sorry about Alex's death. How are you h-ho-holding up?"

"I'm holding up just fine. I'm grieving, of course, but mostly I'm angry, and there's nothing like anger to put iron in a person's spine."

William's own spine stiffened. "Colonel Dudley thinks that Dolan will offer you at least thirty thousand dollars for your store in Lincoln. He will try to c-c-convince you to use that money to buy my way out of this prison. Do not do it."

Susan looked ashen-faced, her mouth a large O. "But

William, I couldn't—"

"You keep fighting the Dolans and the Dudleys of this world. I will take care of myself. P-p-promise me." William put down the bowl of beans.

"I can fight them better with you out of jail," Susan said. "It would be good use of my money to see that happen."

"I am done with being a g-g-gunfighter. You would just be wasting your m-m-money." He pressed Susan's hand. "Besides, I am sure Dolan and Dudley are in this together. Dolan pays you the thirty thousand your store is worth; you give the cash to Dudley, who splits it with Dolan. You lose your store—Dolan gets it for only fifteen thousand and it is all legal."

"I'll never sell to Dolan. So I won't have the money Dudley wants. I'm glad you understand." She smiled at William. "I've wired the president for help, practically daily. I hope that someday soon we'll see justice in Lincoln County."

"I hope you are r-r-right about justice coming to the county, but I do not think I will be here to see it."

"Have faith, William." Susan picked up the empty bowl, replaced it in the basket, and left.

Faith in what, William wondered. Faith in a God that leaves cripples in his wake? Faith in his guns that made him a killer? Faith in Susan's plea to the president?

His last chance for freedom had just walked out the door. He felt at peace. He welcomed the night rats.

*   *   *

In the morning, Dudley came again, this time with five soldiers. "I know you had a chat with Mrs. McSween last evening. Any progress on securing your release?"

"She does not have the money."

"I will wait another day for her to get it." Dudley's voice quivered and rose in pitch.

"She will not be securing my release. That h-h-horse is out of the remuda."

"One more day," Dudley said, then turned on his heel and left. The other soldiers followed him like water down a gutter.

Time crawled in the dark cell, measured by the strip of light that filtered through the high window and inched across the floor. When the brass notes of a bugle called the soldiers to formation, he estimated the time as late morning.

Later he thought he heard shouting outside, though the thick walls made the sound indistinct.

The strip of light crawled another few inches over the floor. A cockroach ventured across the illumination, scuttling from one dark place to another.

The heavy tread of boots in the corridor brought William to the door. He peered out.

Dudley, face flushed and eyes straining, stared back. He held a ring of keys in his hand. Four soldiers, giving each other furtive glances, stood behind the colonel.

William took a step back from the cell door. A key grated in the lock and heavy tumblers tripped. The door opened, hinges screaming in protest.

Dudley stood framed in the opening; the soldiers crowded behind him, forming a semicircle of faces peering over the martinet's shoulder.

"I can't wait any longer," Dudley said. "I need that thirty thousand."

"I do not have it."

"Then I will have to settle for the ten thousand. It's better than nothing." Dudley drew his sidearm and pointed it at William.

"Murder, Colonel?" William pointed at the soldiers. "In front of witnesses? Hoot."

"Yes. Witnesses, but not to murder. To a gunfight."

"You are going to g-g-give me a gun?"

Dudley snorted his little pig laugh. "Of course not." He drew a bead on William's chest.

All this worry and effort to lay down his gun and at the end the choice is taken from him. At peace, William smiled and raised his hands. "At least I die knowing that I was never beaten."

"Maybe, but that'll be our little secret."

Dudley cocked the hammer.

The Last Bullet

"Hold it!" Someone out of William's view called from the end of the corridor. "I want an explanation, Colonel."

William didn't recognize the voice, but Colonel Dudley's expression fell through confidence to indecision to despair. He looked like a man who had just seen his full house beaten by slow-rolled four deuces.

Biting his lip, Dudley eased the hammer down, reholstered his revolver, and turned to face the speaker. "General Wallace, sir." He snapped his hand to touch his brow, palm flat.

A general? Where did he come from? William released the breath he didn't realize he was holding. Squeezing closer to the bars, he squinted around them.

The soldiers behind Dudley backed away as someone approached. Dudley himself took a step back, leaving an open space in front of the cell door.

A portly man with a long, bushy mustache and beard stepped up and peered into the cell. The general's uniform fit him well, making his girth an asset. The chiseled lines of his mouth set in righteous condemnation, though inquisitive amusement played in his eyes.

"Who are you?" the general asked.

"Hoot." William gripped the window bars with both hands, his legs as loose as wet rawhide.

The general gaped at him.

"That's William, my patient," Doctor Stone said, sliding into view beside the general. "I've been asking to see him, but Colonel Dudley denied me access."

"What's he doing in jail?"

"Sir, I am holding him on a charge of criminal trespassing," Dudley said.

"Did you deny him medical care?" The question thundered in the echoing hallway.

"He didn't need any, sir. He's always like that."

General Wallace gave Dudley a scathing look. "You were about to murder him."

"He's a wanted man, sir." Dudley's voice shook.

"He is not a wanted man," Marshal McAdams said. "Not by the law. The colonel wanted to collect a private bounty. Check the telegram in his pocket."

Marshal McAdams—here? William wondered who else still standing in the wings had broken in on his near-execution.

General Wallace held a palm out to the colonel. "Let me see it."

Dudley reached into the inner pocket of his uniform and withdrew a folded paper. He clenched his jaw and handed the missive to the general.

After a brief perusal, the general handed the telegram to McAdams. "Let's adjourn to Colonel Dud—my office and sort this out. Release the prisoner, Colonel, and bring him." General Wallace turned smartly on his heel and strode out.

Strength returned to William's knees. A soldier unlocked the cell, and with a twitch and a grimace, William joined Stone and McAdams. As they followed the soldiers, William asked, "Who is General Wallace?"

"General Lew Wallace," Doctor Stone said. "He presided over the trial of the conspirators in President Lincoln's assassination."

"President Hayes sent him here to look into *this* Lincoln matter," McAdams said. "I told you the government in Washington was coming. Just a matter of time after Mrs. McSween sent her telegrams."

"The t-t-timing could not have been closer."

McAdams glanced at General Wallace, who still had his back to them as he led the way to Dudley's office. The marshal handed the telegram to William. "Read this while you have the chance."

William unfolded the telegram.

TEN THOUSAND DOLLARS PAID ON PROOF THAT YOU KILLED GUNMAN WILLIAM IN PUBLIC GUN-FIGHT STOP REPLY LAW OFFICES WASHBURN AND WASHBURN MIDDLEBORO MASS

Smiling, he handed the paper back to McAdams. "This answers a lot of questions."

Susan McSween waited in the vestibule of Colonel Dudley's office.

She hurried to William. "Are you all right? I was worried. I feared Colonel Dudley was up to something. When General—"

William touched her lightly on the arm. "I am fine. Thanks to you. You s-s-saved my life."

General Wallace ordered Dudley to stand at attention and sat in the colonel's chair. "Now let's sort all this out." He turned to the sergeant who had been Colonel Dudley's aide. "Keep a written record of these proceedings.

"I am General Lew Wallace. The newspapers in the East call the road through Lincoln the 'most dangerous street in

America.' I have been sent under the authority of President Hayes to bring an end to the hostilities. I have wide-ranging powers to do so, up to and including replacing Axtell and becoming the new governor of New Mexico.

"I shall begin my investigation with you, Colonel Dudley."

*　*　*

William relaxed in Doctor Stone's office, enjoying the evening meal with Susan McSween, the doctor, and Marshal McAdams.

"Well begun is well done," Susan said. "I have faith in this general."

"At least he l-l-let me out of prison."

"Because you didn't murder anyone, William," McAdams said. "I believe General Wallace is inclined to call everything even, a clean slate for everyone, to stop this violence. But he won't forgive cold-blooded murder."

"I hope he puts a stop to the gunfighting." Susan took a sip of her coffee.

"That will not happen until the l-l-lawyers Washburn and Washburn withdraw their bounty on me. That is not related to this Lincoln County war, so I doubt the general will be much help."

Slicing his steak, McAdams said, "I'm sure the general

won't hinder you either, so long as you stay within the law."

"Send the Washburns a letter, explain things to them," Doctor Stone said.

"I thought of that. Writing letters is n-n-new to me. I am more used to the sword than the p-p-pen. If I write something, would you three look it over for me? Offer suggestions?"

"Of course," Susan said. "Whenever you're ready."

After dinner William scratched out a message on paper supplied by Doctor Stone.

Dear Mr. Washburn and family,

I am so very sorry for the loss of Mr. Kendrick Washburn, but I did not kill him. I had only just met your relative and liked him. I hoped we would become friends. His loss, I know, is a great blow to your family.

Kendrick was killed by a hired gun who mistook him for me. I killed the man that murdered him. Kendrick's death was a tragic mistake, but such things happen when men hire guns to do their killing for them.

I hope that you can find peace knowing that the man responsible for Kendrick's death has paid for his crime. In all fairness I ask that you withdraw the bounty on me. If you wish to meet personally, I am at your service.

William

Fort Sumner, New Mexico

He handed it to Susan, who looked it over. Her face broke out in a wide smile.

"Why, William, it's perfect. I believe you have a future with a pen when you hang up your gun."

McAdams took the letter from her and read it as well. "Write a second copy and I'll send it to the sheriff—or whatever passes for one in Middleboro, Massachusetts—and enlist his aid to make sure the message gets through."

"Splendid," Doctor Stone said. "Hopefully that'll take care of the problem. You should be home free, William."

They forgot Jesse, William thought, but said, "I hope so." He stood up and tottered as he stretched his lanky frame. "I will feel better when the letters have been delivered."

* * *

William stayed in Fort Sumner the next week and went back to work for Emmett at the stable. A chastised Colonel Dudley awaited his retirement at the fort and kept away from William.

William was feeding the horses one afternoon when McAdams dropped by.

"News from Santa Fe." McAdams struck a match on the door frame and lit a cigar. He held a second tobacco-wrapped cylinder out to William.

William shook his head. He waited until McAdams

drew a deep draught through his cigar before he asked, "What news?"

"Governor Axtell is out. Fired. General Wallace is now the governor."

William picked up a shovelful of grain and threw it into the manger. "That is a good start."

"There's more." McAdams drew in another long draught, eyes twinkling as he watched William.

William shrugged and loaded the shovel again. McAdams would tell him eventually. If good news, it can wait. If bad, it can wait even longer.

"Governor Wallace declared amnesty for everyone, except those accused of murder."

"Billy predicted that would h-h-happen, before any of this even started."

McAdams grew serious. "Only two men were denied amnesty. Ironic, then, that Billy is one of them."

The shovel seemed to weigh an extra twenty pounds. "Why?"

"Because of the murders of Morton, Baker, and Brady."

William nodded. He had been right to be careful to stay within the law. Or, because of that fat corporal, was he the other unpardoned one? But if he were, McAdams wouldn't be smiling. "Who is the other one?"

"Jesse Evans. He has to answer for the murder of Alex McSween."

"Then my f-f-feud with Jesse is over as well." William took a deep breath. The breeze was light, and the air smelled wonderful. He took off his gun belts and hung them on a peg. "I feel fifty pounds lighter. Not that I was afraid I would ever lose, but I am tired of the killing."

McAdams sighed. "No gunfighter ever thinks he's going to lose. That last bullet is always a surprise." His face blossomed into a broad grin. "Doctor Stone and Mrs. McSween are having dinner with me tonight. Please join us."

William passed the afternoon in the rhythmic muscular work of a stable hand. His chores over, he splashed some water on his face, changed to his other shirt, and quite famished, hastened to meet the marshal as invited.

John Chisum, looking to re-establish beef contracts with the army, had stopped by to talk with McAdams. The marshal invited him to the table as well. The amnesty offer dominated the conversation.

"I don't know what has happened to my husband's body," Susan said. She rubbed the bridge of her nose, chasing a tear. "Does this amnesty mean it is safe for me to return to Lincoln? There is also the matter of the store. Without it, I have no income."

"It might be too soon for the aggrieved parties to confront each other," McAdams said. "Amnesty or not." His eyes locked with William's.

"Surely she can't go to Lincoln without an escort,"

Doctor Stone said. "Who else but William will suit?"

The pleasant breeze blowing through William's thoughts all afternoon turned dry and brittle. "I have hung up my guns."

"My business in Lincoln is pressing," Susan said. "But I wouldn't ask you to go back to being a gunfighter, William. Not now that you have a chance to leave it behind."

Chisum leaned back in his chair and folded his arms across his chest. "I was not a party to this Lincoln fighting, and I have friends there I want to see. I'll be glad to escort the lady." He turned to smile at Susan. "If you'll allow me."

Susan frowned. "Are you sure you want to get involved in this trouble?"

Chisum's smile was as broad as Texas. "I'll take four or five of my men with us. There won't be any trouble."

And that was that. With those few words, William felt all his problems evaporate like puddles after a summer downpour. No longer a gunfighter. He'd stay around Fort Sumner for a while, keep working for Emmett.

McAdams served apple pie for dessert, and William thought it the sweetest taste since Kansas.

Susan McSween left town with John Chisum, and William worked at the stable. Two days later Emmett was demonstrating some tricks with rope knots when a boy interrupted. The lad was no more than ten and gaped at the two men, twisting his broad-brimmed hat in his hands.

"What can I do for you, son?" Emmett asked.

"The marshal asked me to come fetch Mr. William," the youngster said, looking squarely at William. "And he said you'd best bring your gun."

William smiled at Emmett's quizzical look. "Probably heard something about Jesse." He took the gun belt that held his Peacemaker from the peg. He did not strap it on, just slung it over his shoulder. He gave Sunfish a pat on the neck. "Be back soon."

William left the lad with Emmett and ambled to the marshal's office.

McAdams sat at his desk, reading handbills, when William walked in. The marshal looked up, eyebrows raised. "Mornin', William. What's up?"

William's breath accelerated and his stomach churned. "You sent for me?"

McAdams pushed back from his desk. "No. Why are you carrying a gun belt?"

"Some boy came to Emmett's and said you w-w-wanted to see me. And I should bring my gun."

"I didn't send for you."

Why would somebody want him in the marshal's of-fice? A trap? William crouched and turned to look out the window. The street's activity looked normal.

As if reading his mind, McAdams asked, "If this was a trap, why ask you to bring your gun?"

"Why does somebody want me in your office?"

"Maybe they wanted you away from the stable, and my office was the only place they figured you'd go without question."

"Leaves the same questions. Who and why."

"Dunno." McAdams shrugged. "Nothing unusual happening in town this morning."

Studying the street, William saw the boy from Emmett's walking toward him. "I think we are about to find out."

The marshal rose from his desk and looked out the window. His brow furrowed, he laid a hand on William's arm. "You stay here. I'll go see what this is about."

Nodding, William laid his gun belt on the marshal's desk. Outside, he heard the creak of the boardwalk as McAdams strode on it.

In a voice that quivered through several octaves, the boy said, "The man in the stable asked me to bring this note to Mr. William." He held up a folded paper.

"You mean Emmett?"

"No, sir. The other man in the stable. The one with the guns."

The boy looked through the window at William. "Marshal, sir, please give this to Mr. William." The lad, hands shaking, gave the note to McAdams, turned, and ran off.

McAdams brought the note to William, who unfolded it while the marshal crowded behind to read over his shoulder.

William, I've got your friend Emmet tied up.
Meet me in front of the stable in five minutes or he dies.
Wear your guns.
   —Jesse

McAdams swore. "So Jesse's in town. The fool. I'll arrest him first chance."

"That will not help Emmett." William looked at his gun belt lying across the desk. Not again.

"No one will blame you," McAdams said, following William's gaze. "Jesse's a wanted outlaw who's threatening to kill an innocent man."

"Not worried about blame." William clenched his hands at his side. "This is how it begins. Jesse started it the first time; put a gun in my hand, and no one blamed me then either. But I have been known as a gunfighter ever since. Such a thing follows you. For the last two days I have known peace and happiness. I knew Jesse was out there, but for once, I did not have to handle things. I trusted the l-l-law."

"Then let the law handle it." McAdams adjusted his gun belt, fastened the holster's tie-down to his leg.

William shook his head. "I have to f-f-face him. I owe it to Emmett. I was wrong to think someone else could settle my account with Jesse." He strapped on his belt, checked the load in the Peacemaker.

McAdams turned toward the back door. "I'll circle around. If you can keep Jesse busy, I'll slip in the back and free Emmett. Then if Jesse is still on his feet, I'll arrest him."

William said, "I swear to you this is the last time I settle things with a gun."

"Sure, William. You'd better get going; the five minutes are up. Keep Jesse busy as long as you can. If this works, you won't even have to fire." McAdams hurried out the back door.

William stepped into the street. A crowd had gathered; even soldiers from the fort lounged in groups along the way. He caught a glimpse of Doctor Stone. Word must have gotten around.

His chest lightened that Susan McSween wasn't there.

Excited faces watched him pass: blood heated by the prospect of death. Most men go their whole lives and never see a person killed, even out west. Well, not counting the war.

Was there some way to handle this without killing? He was willing to let Jesse go, but once again, the man forced his hand. This time it would be done differently. Maybe shoot the gun out of Jesse's hand? William was good, but that good? Even if he died, it made a fair trade so long as Jesse was arrested and stopped.

He neared the stable. Built like a barn, the front had a large double door, only one side of which stood open. Jesse stood off center in that open door, close to the hinged side. Behind him, dark shadows.

"William," Jesse called. "I've arranged for a crowd, as you can see." The gunman's stance looked well balanced; his arms hung loose at his sides.

"You are wasting your time," William shouted, hoping that the crowd would hear as well. "There is no bounty for me anymore, witnesses or no witnesses."

Jesse frowned. "Too bad. I was countin' on that for traveling money."

"So there is no reason to shoot with me. Let Emmett go."

Jesse's hand inched toward his gun. "Do you know they want to arrest me? Take me to prison? I'd rather you kill me than that."

William laughed. "I spent a couple of days in federal custody myself. And I agree with you. Death is preferable." Jesse's arrest was enough to settle the score for John and Alex—and Emily.

But how about the life Jesse forced him into? Jesse could have stopped Walt in Wichita all those years ago.

But he didn't. Was prison enough payback for setting him up to live as a gunfighter?

"C'mon, William, draw." Jesse's face went slack. "C'mon, clown."

Behind Jesse, William saw Emmett creeping forward, a shovel held in his hands like a club. If only William could keep Jesse's attention.

William lowered his hands to his gun belt—and unbuckled it. He let it fall to the ground and stepped away. He steeled his nerves, determined to stand straight without jerking or falling. "You put the first gun in my hand, Jesse. Except for that, I probably would never have picked one up. I blame you for the life I have lived since then, but I am done with it. You said a gunman never gives up his guns. Well, I have—three times now. So I guess I am no gunman."

"Pick up your gun or I'll shoot you where you stand," Jesse shouted. His hand swept toward the revolver in his holster.

The tornado erupted in William's mind, though his hands remained clenched at his side.

In the midst of the maelstrom, in that place of perfect clarity where time stopped while his aim usually locked unfailingly on target, William saw his future flash before his eyes.

Jesse's gun cleared its holster.

Black stains encircled the muzzle like a black eye. Its malevolent gaze locked on William.

William's hand slid to his hip. Glad he had dropped his gun, or he would have drawn and fired in spite of his determination not to.

Shovel poised, Emmett, another low ace, crept through the shadows.

Jesse's gun rose.

Emmett's shovel fell.

William bet it all.

Smoke erupted from Jesse's gun.

"Hoot." William clutched his chest and crumpled into the dirt.

Epilogue

Fort Sumner sweltered in the hot July sun. People stayed in the shadows when they could. No one visited the cemetery.

Emmett worked the stable alone again. He continued to feed Sunfish, treating the horse to an extra carrot or apple when he could spare them.

Doctor Stone inspected William, who was sprawled on the examining table. Bandages stained with red wine crisscrossed his friend's chest.

"How do those feel? Too tight?"

William shook his head. "I have been cooped up here for three days. Are they necessary?"

"They are if you want people to continue to think you're at death's door. Rumors of Jesse shooting you in a gunfight are probably all the way to Santa Fe by now."

"Jesse knows different."

Stone shrugged. "He's not sure what he knows after Emmett gave him that crack on the skull. Anyway, he's in federal custody now, on his way to prison. He was cursing all the way out of town."

Stone handed William his shirt. "Put this on, and remember to pretend to wince when you move."

"Not sure I know the d-d-difference between a wince and my usual." William slid the shirt over the bandages.

Doctor Stone asked, "So, before Emmett spoiled the shot, do you think Jesse was really trying to kill you, or just goad you into fighting back?"

"His first shot was a goad. But he was d-d-desperate, and if he could not force me to shoot him, then there would have been a second shot. He m-m-meant to kill me before they took him off to prison. When I saw Emmett coming up behind him, the idea came to me to l-l-let him kill me. Apparently."

"Good thing I was the first to reach you, or your little charade would have been for naught."

"I counted on you running to help an injured man, while everyone else had eyes only for McAdams's capture of Jesse."

"I say you were damn lucky."

"Yeah, the kind of luck a man cannot count on twice.

This is my chance to leave this gunfighting business behind me, and I am taking it. How long do we have to carry on with this playacting?"

Stone sighed. "We have to get you off the post somehow." He winked. "I predict you'll take a turn for the worse after supper. So sad, to die so young and all." He glanced at the window. "You slip out of town with Sunfish in the dead of night. I'll have Emmett bring a coffin, and he, McAdams, and I will fill it with rocks and bury it tomorrow."

"Will you tell Mrs. McSween the truth?" William asked, fiddling with his shirt buttons.

"Better she not know. Sort of a twist on that witticism 'two people can keep a secret if one of them stays dead.'"

William wondered if she'd be sad. "I worry about her."

"She's been through a lot. She lost her store and found her husband in a dirty blanket tossed in a hole in his own backyard."

William frowned. "What is going to happen to her?"

"When she left, Emily Tunstall gave her the ranch, and now Chisum has taken her under his wing and leases the spread from her. I hear she's planning to keep fighting—in an honest court this time. Dudley and Dolan will have a lot to answer for before she's through."

Doctor Stone opened a trunk in the corner of the room and brought out a carpetbag. "Almost forgot. Susan found this in the bunkhouse and sent it to me, asked me what to do with it."

William laughed. "The bag I brought from Trinidad. Time to pack it once more." He picked up his gun belt, held it as if weighing it.

Doctor Stone folded his hands. "You can leave that here."

William withdrew the Peacemaker from the holster and handed it to the doctor. "This is the gun Jesse gave me. That is all over now." He picked up the double-action revolver. "John Tunstall gave me this one." He slipped it into the carpetbag. "I will keep it in his memory."

"Where will you go?"

"Somewhere peaceful. Away from New Mexico. Arizona m-m-maybe."

"Arizona? William, it's worse than New Mexico."

"Hoot."

THE END

Author's Note

The Clown William series includes real-life characters, settings, and circumstances from the American Old West.

Jesse Evans and William Bonney (aka Billy the Kid) were well-known gunfighters, and Billy's escape from Lincoln, New Mexico, after a leg wound is historically correct. In Lincoln, Dr. Woods, Dolan, Baker, Morton, and Hill were historically based, and Sheriff Brady's death, as well as the fates of the McSweens, occurred as depicted.

John Chisum was a real-life Texas rancher and beef supplier. He is not to be confused with another famous Texan, Jesse Chisholm, who founded the Chisholm Trail to drive cattle from Texas to Kansas.

At Fort Sumner, Colonel Dudley made a real-life appearance, and Governor Axtell's administration was known for its shady dealings, just as portrayed. General/Governor Lew Wallace did become governor of the New Mexico territory and, while in office, wrote the book *Ben-Hur*. (I wonder what that book would have been like had he really met William?)

Kendrick Washburn—the reporter from the first book—was based on a real person, but I changed his profession and the circumstances of his death for dramatic effect. Understandably upset by Kendrick's death, the family did make inquiries—but never placed a bounty on anyone. On the return to Trinidad, Colorado, two other history-inspired characters appear: Dave Rodabaugh (spelled Rudabaugh in real life) and Sheriff Woolton (loosely based on R. L. Wootton). Under the sherriff, Trinidad was known for its relative lawlessness until 1882 when Bat Masterson became marshal.

Mr. Barlow was a partner in the Barlow and Sanderson Stage Company. He retired in 1878, shortly after William's second visit to Trinidad, and he would have denied it had anything to do with William's search for him. After Barlow's departure, the stage company was renamed J. L. Sanderson and Company, which maintained Colorado operations until 1884.

And since the Old West is also a prominent character in William's story, it is noteworthy that the Atchison, Topeka and Santa Fe route bypassed Santa Fe due to construction challenges, and years later, a spur line was put in from Lamy.

In the next book in the series, I tackle the gunfight at the O.K. Corral. The challenge is staying true to history while inserting a fictional character into what is probably the most well-reported and documented gunfight in the Wild West. I hope you enjoy my solution.

About the Author

Robin Elno is a retired army colonel, semiretired psychiatrist, and full-time author. He lives in San Antonio, Texas, where he is an active member of the San Antonio Writers' Guild. Elno's Clown William series was inspired by the work of neurologist Oliver Sacks, who wrote about the unusual speed and accuracy often displayed by people with Tourette's syndrome. Intrigued by the idea that strengths can rise from differences, Elno created the unique and compelling character of Clown William. Elno's novels are often set against true historical backdrops like the Wild West.

We delight in publishing the non-traditional, unconventional and alternative including:

Fiction
Metaphysical
Professional and Nonfiction
Romance
Young Adult
IE Snaps!

Review our list of themes and topics and perhaps they will inspire you to consider writing for original genres and audiences.

www.ingramelliott.com